Black Juice

Black Juice

Margo Lanagan

GOLLANCZ
LONDON

The right of Margo Lanagan to be identified as the author
of this work has been asserted by her in accordance with the
Copyright, Designs and Patents Act 1988.

First published in Great Britain in 2006 by
Gollancz
An imprint of the Orion Publishing Group
Orion House, 5 Upper St Martin's Lane, London
WC2H 9EA

A CIP catalogue record for this book
is available from the British Library

EAN 9780575077812
ISBN 0 575 07781 6

10 9 8 7 6 5 4 3 2

Typeset at The Spartan Press Ltd,
Lymington, Hants

Printed in Great Britain by
Mackays of Chatham, PLC

www.orionbooks.co.uk

contents

singing my sister down

We all went down to the tar-pit, with mats to spread our weight.

Ikky was standing on the bank, her hands in a metal twin-loop behind her. She'd stopped sulking; now she looked, more, stare-y and puzzled.

Chief Barnarndra pointed to the pit. 'Out you go then, girl. You must walk on out there to the middle and stand. When you picked a spot, your people can join you.'

So Ik stepped out, very ordinary. She walked out. I thought – hoped, even – she might walk right across and into the thorns the other side; at the same time, I knew she wouldn't do that.

She walked the way you walk on the tar, except without the arms balancing. She nearly fell from a stumble once, but Mumma hulloo'd to her, and she straightened and walked upright out to the very middle, where she slowed and stopped.

Mumma didn't look to the chief, but all us kids and the rest did. 'Right, then,' he said.

Mumma stepped out as if she'd just herself that moment happened to decide to. We went after her – only us, Ik's

3

family, which was like us being punished, too, everyone watching us walk out to that girl who was our shame.

In the winter you come to the pit to warm your feet in the tar. You stand long enough to sink as far as your ankles – the littler you are, the longer you can stand. You soak the heat in for as long as the tar doesn't close over your feet and grip, and it's as good as warmed boots wrapping your feet. But in summer, like this day, you keep away from the tar, because it makes the air hotter and you mind about the stink.

But today we had to go out, and everyone had to see us go.

Ikky was tall, but she was thin and light from all the worry and prison; she was going to take a long time about sinking. We got our mats down, all the food parcels and ice-baskets and instruments and such spread out evenly on the broad planks Dash and Felly had carried out.

'You start, Dash,' said Mumma, and Dash got up and put his drum-ette to his hip and began with 'Fork-Tail Trio', and it did feel a bit like a party. It stirred Ikky awake from her hung-headed shame; she lifted up and even laughed, and I saw her hips move in the last chorus, side to side.

Then Mumma got out one of the ice-baskets, which was already black on the bottom from meltwater.

Ikky gasped. 'Ha! What! Crab! Where'd that come from?'

'Never you mind, sweet-thing.' Mumma lifted some meat to Ikky's mouth, and rubbed some of the crush-ice into her hair.

'Oh, Mumma!' Ik said with her mouth full.

'May as well have the best of this world while you're here,' said Mumma. She stood there and fed Ikky like a baby, like a pet guinea-bird.

'I thought Auntie Mai would come,' said Ik.

'Auntie Mai, she's useless,' said Dash. 'She's sitting at home with her handkerchief.'

'I wouldn't've cared, her crying,' said Ik. 'I would've thought she'd say goodbye to me.'

'Her heart's too hurt,' said Mumma. 'You frightened her. And she's such a straight lady – she sees shame where some of us just see people. Here, inside the big claw, that's the sweetest meat.'

'Ooh, *yes*! Is anyone else feasting with me?'

'No, darlin', this is your day only. Well, okay, I'll give some to this little sad-eyes here, huh? Felly never had crab but the once. Is it yum? Ooh, it's yum! Look at him!'

Next she called me to do my flute – the flashiest, hardest music I knew. And Ik listened; Ik who usually screamed at me to stop pushing spikes into her brain, she watched my fingers on the flute-holes and my sweating face and my straining, bowing body and, for the first time, I didn't feel like just the nuisance-brother. I played well, out of the surprise of her not minding. I couldn't've played better. I heard everyone else being surprised, too, at the end of those tunes that they must've known, too well from all my practising.

I sat down, very hungry. Mumma passed me the water cup and a damp-roll.

'I'm stuck now,' said Ik, and it was true – the tar had her by the feet, closed in a gleaming line like that pair of zipper-slippers I saw once in the shoemaster's vitrine.

'Oh yeah, well and truly stuck,' said Mumma. 'But then, you knew when you picked up that axe-handle you were sticking yourself.'

'I did know.'

'No coming unstuck from this one. You could've let that handle lie.'

That was some serious teasing.

'No, I couldn't, Mumma, and *you* know.'

'I do, baby chicken. I always knew you'd be too angry, once the wedding-glitter rubbed off your skin. It was a good party, though, wasn't it?' And they laughed at each other, Mumma having to steady Ikky or her ankles would've snapped over. And when their laughter started going strange Mumma said, 'Well, *this* party's going to be almost as good, 'cause it's got children. And look what else!' And she reached for the next ice-basket.

And so the whole long day went, in treats and songs, in ice and stink and joke-stories and gossip and party-pieces. On the banks, people came and went, and the chief sat in his chair and was fanned and fed, and the family of Ikky's husband sat around the chief, being served, too, all in purple-cloth with flashing edging, very prideful.

She went down so slowly.

'Isn't it hot?' Felly asked her.

'It's like a big warm hug up my legs,' said Ik. 'Come here and give me a hug, little stick-arms, and let me check. Oof, yes, it's just like that, only lower down.'

'You're coming down to me,' said Fel, pleased.

'Yeah, soon I'll be able to bite your ankles like you bite mine.'

Around midafternoon, Ikky couldn't move her arms any more and had a panic, just quiet, not so the bank-people would've noticed.

'What'm I going to do, Mumma?' she said. 'When it comes up over my face? When it closes my nose?'

'Don't you worry. You won't be awake for that.' And Mumma cooled her hands in the ice, dried them on her dress, and rubbed them over Ik's shoulders, down Ik's arms to where the tar had locked her wrists.

'You better not give me any teas, or herbs, or anything,' said Ik. 'They'll get you, too, if you help me. They'll come out to make sure.'

Mumma put her hands over Felly's ears. 'Tristem gave me a gun,' she whispered.

Ikky's eyes went wide. 'But you can't! Everyone'll hear!'

'It's got a thing on it, quietens it. I can slip it in a tar-wrinkle, get you in the head when your head is part sunk, fold back the wrinkle, tell 'em your heart stopped, the tar pressed it stopped.'

Felly shook his head free. Ikky was looking at Mumma, quietening. There was only the sound of Dash tearing bread with his teeth, and the breeze whistling in the thorn-galls away over on the shore. I was watching Mumma and Ikky closely – I'd wondered about that last part, too. But now this girl up to her waist in the pit didn't even look like our Ikky. Her face was changing like a cloud, or like a masque-lizard's colours; you don't see them move but they *become* something else, then something else again.

'No,' she said, still looking at Mumma. 'You won't do that. You won't have to.' Her face had a smile on it that touched off one on Mumma's, too, so that they were both quiet, smiling at something in each other that I couldn't see.

And then their eyes ran over and they were crying *and*

smiling, and then Mumma was kneeling on the wood, her arms around Ikky, and Ikky was ugly against her shoulder, crying in a way that we couldn't interrupt them.

That was when I realised how many people were watching, when they set up a big, spooky oolooling and stamping on the banks, to see Mumma grieve.

'Fo!' I said to Dash, to stop the hair creeping around on my head from that noise. 'There never was such a crowd when Chep's daddy went down.'

'Ah, but he was old and crazy,' said Dash through a mouthful of bread, 'and only killed other olds and crazies.'

'Are those fish-people? And look at the yellow-cloths – they're from up among the caves, all that way!'

'Well, it's nearly Langasday, too,' said Dash. 'Lots of people on the move, just happening by.'

'Maybe. Is that an honour, or a greater shame?'

Dash shrugged. 'This whole thing is upended. Who would have a party in the tar, and with family going down?'

'It's what Mumma wanted.'

'Better than having her and Ik be like this *all day*.' Dash's hand slipped into the nearest ice-basket and brought out a crumb of gilded macaroon. He ate it as if he had a perfect right.

Everything went slippery in my mind, after that. We were being watched so hard! Even though it was quiet out here, the pothering wind brought crowd-mumble and scraps of music and smoke our way, so often that we couldn't be private and ourselves. Besides, there was Ikky with the sun on her face, but the rest of her from the rib-peaks down gloved in tar, never to see sun again. Time seemed to just have *gone*, in big clumps, or all the day was happening at once or something, I was wondering so hard about what was to come, I was watching so hard the differences from our normal days. I wished I had more time to think, before she went right down; my mind was going breathless, trying to get all its thinking done.

But evening came and Ik was a head and shoulders, singing along with us in the lamplight, all the old songs – 'A Flower for You', 'Hen and Chicken Bay', 'Walking the Tracks with Beejum Singh', 'Dollarberries'. She sang all Felly's little-kid songs that normally she'd sneer at; she got Dash to teach her his new one, 'The Careless Wanderer', with the tricky chorus. She made us work on that one like she was trying to stop us noticing the monster bonfires around the shore, the other singing, of fishing songs and forest songs, the stomp and clatter of dancing in the gathering darkness. But they were there, however well we sang, and no other singing in our lives had had all this going on behind it.

When the tar began to tip Ik's chin up, Mumma sent me for the wreath. 'Mai will have brought it, over by the chief's chair.'

I got up and started across the tar, and it was as if I cast magic ahead of me, silence-making magic, for as I walked – and it was good to be walking, not sitting – musics petered out, and laughter stopped, and dancers stood still, and there were eyes at me, all along the dark banks, strange eyes and familiar both.

The wreath showed up in the crowd ahead, a big, pale ring trailing spirals of whisper-vine, the beautifullest thing. I climbed up the low bank there, and the ground felt hard and cold after a day on the squishy tar. My ankles shivered as I took the wreath from Mai. It was heavy; it was fat with heavenly scents.

'You'll have to carry those,' I said to Mai, as someone handed her the other garlands. 'You should come out, anyway. Ik wants you there.'

She shook her head. 'She's cloven my heart in two with that axe of hers.'

'What, so you'll chop hers as well, this last hour?'

We glared at each other in the bonfire light, all loaded down with the fine, pale flowers.

'I never heard this boy speak with a voice before, Mai,' said someone behind her.

'He's very sure,' said someone else. 'This is Ikky's Last Things we're talking about, Mai. If she wants you to be one of them . . .'

'She shouldn't have shamed us, then,' Mai said, but weakly.

'You going to look back on this and think yourself a po-face,' said the first someone.

'But it's like—' Mai sagged and clicked her tongue. 'She should have *cared* what she did to this family,' she said with her last fight. 'It's more than just herself.'

'Take the flowers, Mai. Don't make the boy do this twice over. Time is short.'

'Yeah, *everybody's* time is short,' said the first someone. Mai stood, pulling her mouth to one side.

I turned and propped the top of the wreath on my forehead, so that I was like a little boy-bride, trailing a head of flowers down my back to the ground. I set off over the tar, leaving the magic silence in the crowd. There was only the rub and squeak of flower stalks in my ears; in my eyes, instead of the flourishes of bonfires, there were only the lamps in a ring around Mumma, Felly, Dash, and Ikky's head. Mumma was kneeling bonty-up on the wood, talking to Ikky; in the time it had taken me to get the wreath, Ikky's head had been locked still.

'Oh, the baby,' Mai whimpered behind me. 'The little darling.'

Bit late for darling-ing now, I almost said. I felt cross and frightened and too grown-up for Mai's silliness.

'Here, Ik, we'll make you beautiful now,' said Mumma, laying the wreath around Ik's head. 'We'll come out here to these flowers when you're gone, and know you're here.'

'They'll die pretty quick – I've seen it.' Ik's voice was getting squashed, coming out through closed jaws. 'The heat wilts 'em.'

'They'll always look beautiful to you,' said Mumma. 'You'll carry down this beautiful wreath, and your family singing.'

I trailed the vines out from the wreath like flares from the edge of the sun.

'Is that Mai?' said Ik. Mai looked up, startled, from laying the garlands between the vines. 'Show me the extras, Mai.'

Mai held up a garland. 'Aren't they good? Trumpets from Low Swamp, Auntie Patti's whisper-vine, and star-weed to bind. You never thought ordinary old stars could look so good, I'll bet.'

'I never did.'

It was all set out right, now. It went in the order: head, half-ring of lamps behind (so as not to glare in her eyes), wreath, half-ring of garlands behind, leaving space in front of her for us.

11

'Okay, we're going to sing you down now,' said Mumma. 'Everybody get in and say a proper goodbye.' And she knelt inside the wreath a moment herself, murmured something in Ikky's ear and kissed her on the forehead.

We kids all went one by one. Felly got clingy and made Ikky cry; Dash dashed in and planted a quick kiss while she was still upset and would hardly have noticed him; Mumma gave me a cloth and I crouched down and wiped Ik's eyes and nose – and then could not speak to her bare, blinking face.

'You're getting good at that flute,' she said.

But this isn't about me, Ik. This is *not at all* about me.

'Will you come out here some time, and play over me, when no one else's around?'

I nodded. Then I had to say some words, of some kind, I knew. I wouldn't get away without speaking. 'If you want.'

'I want, okay? Now give me a kiss.'

I gave her a kid's kiss, on the mouth. Last time I kissed her, it was carefully on the cheek as she was leaving for her wedding. Some of her glitter had come off on my lips. Now I patted her hair and backed away over the wreath.

Mai came in last. 'Fairy doll,' I heard her say sobbingly. 'Only-one.'

And Ik, 'It's all right, Auntie. It'll be over so soon, you'll see. And I want to hear your voice nice and strong in the singing.'

We readied ourselves, Felly in Mumma's lap, then Dash, then me next to Mai. I tried to stay attentive to Mumma, so Mai wouldn't mess me up with her weeping. It was quiet except for the distant flubber and snap of the bonfires.

We started up, all the ordinary evening songs for putting babies to sleep, for farewelling, for soothing broke-hearted people – all the ones everyone knew so well that they'd long ago made rude versions and joke-songs of them. We sang them plain, following Mumma's lead; we sang them straight, into Ikky's glistening eyes, as the tar climbed her chin. We stood tall, so as to see her, and she us, as her face became the sunken centre of that giant flower, the wreath. Dash's little drum held us together and kept us singing, as Ik's eyes rolled and she struggled for breath against the pressing tar, as the chief and the husband's family came and stood across from us, shifting from foot to foot, with torches raised to watch her sink away.

Mai began to crumble and falter beside me as the tar closed in on Ik's face, a slow, sticky, rolling oval. I sang good and strong – I didn't want to hear any last whimper, any stopped breath. I took Mai's arm and tried to hold her together that way, but she only swayed worse, and wept louder. I listened for Mumma under the noise, pressed my eyes shut and made my voice follow hers. By the time I'd steadied myself that way, Ik's eyes were closing.

Through our singing, I thought I heard her cry for Mumma; I tried not to, yet my ears went on hearing. *This will happen only the once – you can't do it over again if ever you feel like remembering.* And Mumma went to her, and I could not tell whether Ik was crying and babbling, or whether it was a trick of our voices, or whether the people on the banks of the tar had started up again. I watched Mumma, because Mumma

13

knew what to do; she knew to lie there on the matting, and dip her cloth in the last water with the little fading fish-scales of ice in it, and squeeze the cloth out and cool the shrinking face in the hole.

And the voice of Ik must have been ours or others' voices, because the hole Mumma was dampening with her cloth was, by her hand movements, only the size of a brassboy now. And by a certain shake of her shoulders I could tell: Mumma knew it was all right to be weeping now, now that Ik was surely gone, was just a nose or just a mouth with the breath crushed out of it, just an eye seeing nothing. And very suddenly it was too much – the flowers nodding in the lamplight, our own sister hanging in tar, going slowly, slowly down like Vanderberg's truck that time, like Jappity's cabin with the old man still inside it, or any old villain or scofflaw of around these parts— and I had a big sicking-up of tears, and they tell me I made an awful noise that frightened everybody right up to the chief, and that the husband's parents thought I was a very ill-brought-up boy for upsetting them instead of allowing them to serenely and superiorly watch justice be done for their lost son.

I don't remember a lot about that part. I came back to myself walking dully across the tar between Mai and Mumma, hand-in-hand, carrying nothing, when I had come out here laden, when we had all had to help. *We must have eaten everything*, I thought. *But what about the mats and pans and planks?* Then I heard a screeking clanking behind me, which was Dash hoisting up too heavy a load of pots.

And Mumma was talking, wearily, as if she'd been going on a long time, and soothingly, which was like a beautiful guide-rope out of my sickness, which my brain was following hand over hand. *It's what they do to people, what they have to do, and all you can do about it is watch out who you go loving, right? Make sure it's not someone who'll rouse that killing-anger in you, if you've got that rage, if you're like our Ik—*

Then the bank came up high in front of us, topped with grass that was white in Mumma's lamp's light. Beyond it were all the eyes, and attached to the eyes the bodies, flat and black against bonfire or starry sky. They shuffled aside for us.

I knew we had to leave Ik behind, and I didn't make a fuss, not now. I had done my fussing, all at once; I had blown myself to bits out on the tar, and now several monstrous things, several gaping mouths of truth, were rattling pieces of me around their teeth. I would be all right, if Mai stayed quiet, if Mumma kept murmuring, if both their hands held me as we passed through this forest of people, these flitting firefly eyes.

They got me up the bank, Mumma and Auntie; I paused and they stumped up and then lifted me, and I walked up the impossible slope like a demon, horizontal for a moment and then stiffly over the top—

—and into my Mumma, whose arms were ready. She couldn't've carried me out on the tar. We'd both have sunk, with me grown so big now. But here on the hard ground she took me up, too big as I was for it. And, too big as I was, I held myself onto her, crossing my feet around her back, my arms behind her neck. And she carried me like Jappity's wife used to carry Jappity's idiot son, and I felt just like that boy, as if the thoughts that were all right for everyone else weren't coming now, and never would come, to me. As if all I could do was watch, but not ever know anything, not ever understand. I pushed my face into Mumma's warm neck; I sealed my eyes shut against her skin; I let her strong warm arms carry me away in the dark.

my lord's man

Mullord rides fast away, to the forest.

'Give me that grey,' I say to Bandy.

Bandy hooks the mare out of the stall, and I'm astride and moving before I've properly had time to think. Mullord is a small patch of darkness rocking through the dusk. Taking the hill path, as I said he would.

'That wagon will slow them,' I told Cook and Gerdie. 'All our master has to do is go over the hills. They'll camp at Tampton, or at Brittly Spring, under the Seat.'

'Not with that prize aboard,' said Cook, all in a shiver of delighted horror. 'Not if they've a brain anywhere among their rags and tattles. Bury theersalluvs in a cave somewheres. Magic theersalluvs right off to Arribee, or further. They could do that, theer kind.'

I can believe it. I can believe Mullord and I are riding out to nothing, to a long night of black nothing, silent country. So outlandish has the day been, and last night, and yesterday, too.

But now all will be well. Mullord is back from his travels, and he knows. Whatever can be put right, Mullord will put it. We needn't twirl our thumbs and worry any longer.

I throw myself low on the grey's neck as we go in among the trees. I know the hill path, but not branch for branch as Mullord does. I might not catch up with him; I might meet the both of them coming back, like that time she set out for her father's hold, in that great temper after they were wed. Yes, I'll meet them like that, hand-in-hand between the horses, their heads together in close-talk, Mullord's face with the look on it, like a warm hand has smoothed off all the sternness.

Except it's night, rushing night, and it hasn't happened yet. And sternness wasn't the word for Mullord when he was told, this evening, as he came in the house-gate. Leermonth and Jamey got to him first, the young bletherers.

'Is this true, Berry?' he said to me as I hurried up.

'About her ladyship? Every word, Mullord.'

I saw, 'twas as he heard it fall from *my* lips that he credited it. Time was when that would have given me pleasure, when I was young and learning the ways of lords; nowadays it's only my due. All it did this time was bring home, like a hammer blow to my chest, how terrible a thing she had done. To all of us through him, to be sure, but mostly to him; what her cruel cold heart had done upon his true one. I saw her for the child she was, for the thoughtless murdering child, in that moment, in Mullord's fallen face.

My cheek is against the grey's mane, my ear listening past our thunder and branch-crack, up to Mullord on the hill ahead. I can hear nothing, but he must not go too fast, must not tire that big black horse, for all it's fresh and kept trim for just this use. Them rag-tags may have gone hell for leather, taken fright once they got out, once they sobered up and saw they had a lord's wife with them.

'Did *none* of ours go with them?' Mullord had raged, striding to the stables.

'Mullady wouldn't let us,' I said. 'She cast a pot at Minnow's head, who would go with her. The woman's been senseless these many hours since, and the leech don't hold out hope for her. After that, only the little handmaid would go, and she came back weeping, at noon-tide, saying Mistress had spoken harsh to her and would not have her near.'

I did not like the look of him, the darting eyes, the snarl on his mouth. If she had meant to send him mad by this, I thought she had perhaps succeeded. And I did not want to see such a noble mind turning.

And then Bandy was before us with the coalblack saddled and bridled, and Mullord walked straight up onto its back, and off he rode.

I come out onto the bald hilltop, and in the freedom from branch-thwackings I hear him ahead, well ahead, turmoiling up the next hill. He doesn't need me; his rage and power will alone accomplish whatever he intends. But could I bear to go back to the keep, and gaze at wall and window? Better to be out and moving, even fruitlessly, than sitting wondering, stilling servants' chatter. And I would go after him as I would not go after his wife; I'm his, not hers, as I've said to Gerdie many a time.

'Get you,' says my wife, her eyes laughing. 'One kind word from her and you'd be theirs both.'

'And I might,' I rally, 'but the mistress is hardly one for kindness, is she?'

'She isn't one for anything much,' says my Gerd. 'A flash of fire, a prickly bit of lightning. She doesn't know what she herself's about, let alone her lord and his lordship.'

Night falls while we're in the hills, a clear night with no moon yet. I catch up with Mullord spelling his horse, walking the Grey Comb, a shadow in the starlight.

'Berry,' he says as I come up.

'Mullord.'

He's walking purposive, has not lost his stride. I dismount and walk beside, as I can here, trotting a little to keep up. But he does not disburthen himself to me, for the full length of the Comb; he watches his footing and keeps moving, as if she has a hook in his breast and is drawing him to her through the night, and all he can feel is the pain of it, and work and work to ease it.

The Plunge by starlight is a dire place, and not something you hurry. You hold yourself by teeth and ears and your horse's toenails to that cliff, and promise Nature anything if she'll let you out the other side. You ponder nothing but getting step to step; there's no time even to curse the lady who brought you here.

And then I'm wobbling with relief on the flat, and the paler darkness of the road swings out of the trees and into our path, and I think we have a chance again.

My cousin the innkeeper is already out, with a lamp and fresh horses ready.

'You're in luck,' he says. 'They needed a wheelwright. I sent them over Yarrow way to Dipsy Wheeler, but I don't know as they'll make it as far as that.'

'And our lady was among them?' Mullord cuts in.

Cousin's eyes dart aside.

'How was she conducting herself? Tell me true, man. Was she upright?'

'She was upright and . . . she was singing, Mullord.'

'Had they plied her with wine?'

'She-she-she gave every appearance of being sober, sir.' He busies himself with some harness-straightening at my foot.

'Come, Berry,' says Mullord, and kicks his horse into a trot.

My cousin stands back and casts me a look that says, *Didn't we all know it would come to this?* and it's off with us into the night again.

Heaven Seat pushes its stony shoulders up out of the forest beside us. Mullord disappears into the trees, and my mare follows him. I keep my head down and see almost nothing until we reach the place where we leave the horses. Even walking up to the Seat, there's only the master's shape striding against tangle upon darker tangle. When we clear the brush, the starlight makes me squint after such close darkness, and the breeze is sudden and cold.

She always drew your eye to her, did the mistress. There at the edge of the farmlands spilling along the valley floor, in the golden whirl of the rag-tags' camp, that's her dancing, that's the spinning, sparkling skirt of her. There are other women, of course, but none have cause to move so fiercely. Tiny shouts come up to us, miniature cheers, scrapings of music, fine as crickets' wheezing.

And Mullord pauses. I thought he would cry her name out and rage down the hill, dagger drawn. I thought he'd be set afire by the final sight of her, after all this riding, after all this strife. But he pauses, and seems blind, the gleam of their distant camp in both his gazing eyes.

'Will we go down, sir?' I say, at last.

There's time for a reel to finish, a round of gleeful cries, the fiddler to tune up and another faster dance to begin, before he speaks. 'Yes, Berry, we'll go down. But slowly, silently.'

'You want to surprise them, sir?'

'I'll do nothing yet.'

We slip back into the dark brush, and cross the road at the Seat's foot, into the more open forest. It's a while of walking before we hear the music stronger, before shards and flickers of fire-orange show among the trees. Mullord moves quieter and quieter, until he's like a cat stepping silent through the forest, not snapping twig nor rasping leaf. I stay a little behind him and choose the same quiet places to let my foot fall.

We come up to the camp behind the broken wagon. The music digs fingers into my brain and twirls it like a top. I remember from last night the feverishness of it, fast impatient music that demands new steps of your feet. Those tunes are the only fine thing the rag-tags have – the rest is missing teeth and leathery skin and ruffianly manners.

They've built up a great fire just like the one in the keep courtyard, a great cone twisting to a sparking plume at the top. They're all dancing, from the old toothless ones to the little staggerers jigging and tumbling at the edges. And the mistress is being passed (or passing herself – it's hard to say) from hand to hand around the circle, a whorl within a whorl. Her fine blood shows, and her less fine – she has bearing, but she also has their energy, their not wanting to be bothered with courtliness, with subtle talk and after-you-no-after-you-mullord ways.

I arrive at Mullord's side. He stands like a statue; only the gleams in his eyes move. His hands don't clench; his jaw is not set with rage. What is the man made of, that he can have such outrage before his eyes and be calm? That he can watch his own wife cavort with the rubbish of the earth and keep his temper?

More astounding still, that he can smile! I stare at him. Yes, it's true! It's not just fire-flicker tweaking his mouth, but – what? Mirth? Joy? I hunt and hunt for wryness or bitterness in his face, for poison, for grief. I find none. He might be watching the children's tourney on Midsummer Eve, benign – charmed even.

Rage surges at my throat. Were she my wife— But I chose a good wife, one that would steady me in my youth and companion me in my old age. Mullord, steady in himself from his very beginnings – well, what was he after, taking this wild girl to him? She's ornament enough, but does she care for his holdings and his duty? Does she mind about his people, like a proper lady? I'd swear sometimes he wed her expressly to crumble his keep from within, to stab his right hand with the dagger held in his left.

Mullord steps out of the forest, idly almost, lightly. I strain after him, frightened to follow, frightened of the noisy dancers and of what they will make of him. And he walks forward unnoticed, to the ring of dancers. And he joins them, and begins to hand the women along, just like all the others.

I hold my breath as she comes around to him. I watch for the slight change of his rhythm that will mean he has gone for

his dagger. She will slump to the ground; the whole spell-
bound lot of them will fall into disarray, the music will go on
for a little, until fiddler and drummer see the confusion
and stumble in their rhythm and stop, and then it'll be all
blood and horror, with Mullord in the centre, dealing out the
punishment they so richly deserve.

She comes to him. She twirls. She passes on.

She did not even see him, I think.

And he, he might not care a jot; he reaches for the next
raggy woman in her garish dress, with her eye-paint and her
brass earrings and her mouth like a hole in her face, and he
spins her too, as if she were noble as his lady.

'Strike me!' I'm saying in the bushes. 'Knock me down with
a goose-feather! What's the man up to?'

I keep watching. I think, maybe the third time he'll have
built up rage enough to strike at the minx's heart. But the
third time passes, and the seventh, and the twelfth. All the
magic numbers pass, and then the music changes, and a shout
goes up, and each man takes hold of the woman in front of
him, and some men grasp men and some women women, and
the big circle breaks up into many smaller circles. Mullord, he
isn't lost in there – he's taller, and cleaner of skin, and
smoother-haired than any of them – but he's as lost as a lord
can be among rag-tags, a witch in his arms and his wife in the
arms of a fox-eating thief.

I don't see the moment his lady notices him, whether she
has the grace to startle, or whether she cries out in joy to see
him there, the best of both her worlds dancing at the same
fire. But I see them partnered in the dance, just like gipsies, as
if they care no more and no less for each other than for any of

the mad-caps whirling around them. They move on with no glance back, but give themselves entirely to the next man, the next woman the dance whirls into their path.

But she deserves killing, for what she does to Mullord's heart! She deserves beating at least for stupidity, running away from the finest, wisest lord that ever lived. And here he is – he lets her play, lets her have her way, never shows her the pain she causes him. She dances, and *he dances with her* as if none of it mattered: not her night's carousing in the courtyard of his keep; not her snuffing out the life, perhaps, of good loyal Minnow; not our long ride after her over the hills and down the Plunge—

'Tis *I* who hold the mattering, the bitterness, on his behalf, on behalf of us all. I hold and stir and carry it back and forth among the bushes, until it curdles into a poor kind of sleep. All night I lie where I can lift my head and see the fire and the dancers, where I can hear a change – though no change comes – in the music or the mood, where I can wait in sick discomfort, for morning and for sanity.

As night lifts into the first grey of dawn, I walk the curving road around Heaven Seat. Mullord has gone on ahead to fetch our horses. I'm to walk the mistress – on the keep's best mount, that she helped herself to – around by the road to meet him.

I feel as if I've breakfasted on grit, as if sand has been rubbed into my eyes, as if moss-clumps have been shaken through my clothes and left them damp and itchy. I've dreamed so many endings to these dreadful days, I cannot tell whether this is just more dreaming.

27

And when she speaks, I cannot tell if it's her or my own mind speaking. Her voice is ragged from the long night's singing and smoke.

'You don't care greatly for me, do you, Berry?'

'It is not my place to think of you any particular way, Mistress,' I say, without turning to her.

'I asked you a question; have the grace to answer it.' The voice is soft and rough, and perhaps knows my answer already.

Field and forest are utterly silent around us. It's that moment when the birds pause between waking and heralding the dawn. The road leads us into thicker grey air, full of silty shapes that might become green, might become brown, with time, with light. I search my own grey heart for some truth. It's a long search, while the horse idles along beside me, his great warm head at my shoulder.

The mistress makes some patient movement with her arm, perhaps to push her loosening hair from her eyes. The expensive sound of sleeve against bodice enrages me anew. A dress such as my Gerdie would never dream to wear, the new dress, freshly boned and beaded and trimmed, in which Madam made her first grand entrance into the keep two nights ago, graciously acknowledging the gipsies' yodels of admiration – now that rich dress is singed, and splashed with wine, and its lace-bands are torn off and given to some witch-woman back at the wagon. Hours of work, it will take, to bring it back from such a state, hours Mullord will go sleep-less about his duties, hours the mistress will no doubt sleep away in her feather bed, aware of naught but her own comfort.

I wait to speak, until I know my voice will not shake with

anger. 'Mullord sees something in you,' I finally say, 'beyond your beauty and beyond your rage at the world. If he sees it, I believe it must be there.'

She gives a tiny, mirthless laugh. We round the bend beside the Seat. Up among the trees a horse greets the master with a whinny.

'Continue, Berry.'

'Mistress?'

'My *lord* sees something in me, you say. But does Berry see?' She's not jesting; she's asking me for a piece of myself, without telling me how she'll use it; whether she'll toss it away, and Berry with it, or hold it in her heart to fester and poison my life with.

I stroke the bay's head for comfort. There's no care inside that great skull; nothing will ever come out of those tunnel nostrils, that soft-leather mouth, but grassy air.

'Why, I see the rage, as we all do. And I see the beauty, for no one could miss that either.' That prickle of lightning, which doesn't know its own power.

The tree-shadows muffle nothing – not my voice, not the mistress's fine ears. 'But the other thing – I cannot lie to you, Mistress. I do not see it.'

We wait at the bottom of the path. The sun creaks a little higher at the edge of the world, and I can see the mistress's face composed, raised to the scrubby hillside, her beauty no less for the absence of its usual colour, for the shadows exhaustion has painted around her eyes.

'I will tell you, Berry,' she says, her voice broken to a croak, 'I cannot see that other thing either.'

And in that moment I glimpse it, in that ruefulness, in that bearing. Danced to a rag and faced by only herself in the morning, still she is straight-backed and undiminished.

She turns to me, and a comb from her head tinkles to the road. The hair falls sumptuous on her shoulders, unrolls down her back, pools in her lap. She meets my eye, her face white and cool.

'So we must both trust my lord's sight,' she whispers, 'and hold onto that trust, mustn't we? 'Tis all either of us can do.'

I bend to retrieve the comb. As I straighten, I find myself smiling. I have never looked her full in the face before.

She does not smile back; I never expected that. There won't ever, I don't think, be smiles and kindnesses out of this Mullady. She regards me a moment longer with her shadowed eyes. Then she turns her head, and I turn mine, and we both are still, listening to the master and horses come down the hill.

red nose day

'Have you *gotta* do that?' It was my first time out with Jelly; I was used to quiet.

But Jelly had class, and all the allergies that come with that. He hawked and gobbed in the corner one last time. 'Yeah, or it chokes me. Whaddaya see?'

'When I can *concentrate* . . . nothing yet.'

In the circle of the sights, the wet banner sagged. Of *Jeux des Bouffons*, I could only read *Jex Buffs*, and the face beside it was folded across the middle, so it wasn't even red-nosed.

We were up high, in the nuns' palace. No one had slept here since the old girls got torched for wowserism, so it was a good hide. And it gave this brilliant view of the Lyric. When I took my eyes from the sights, the banner was a faraway blob, the Stage Door light a white pinprick among the buildings; we had *great* distance. No one would ever spot us from down there. And we didn't have to be anywhere near a real buffoon.

The rain was only a spot here and there now, but this morning's storms had given all the gargoyles black beards, and hung drops from every stone leaf and berry. Rain-filled potholes glinted along the streets. We were crouched inside, in a mist of our own breath, the draught chilling our eyeballs. The filthy window was cracked open just wide enough for the muzzle of the Fioreschiacciare.

'She's a beautiful weapon, all right.'

Jelly cocked his head, clicked his tongue in agreement, and kept fumbling in his jacket pockets.

I stroked the curved clips remaining in the canister, awed at myself, how far I'd come. A top-of-the-line Fiore. Famous for her precision work during the Lemonade Wars, she was matt black, with the slender, high-haunched build of all the weapons Benato designed for Fiore. And totally focused on the job – no engraving, no mirror-plating, no fussy walnut work. The only mark on her was the serial number stamped into her barrel.

Jelly dragged out a pouch and papers. I snorted. 'With *your* lungs.'

'Always feel like a ciggy after a good cough. For the dragging feeling.' He flattened a hand to his chest and pulled in a breath of must and fog, pretending to swoon. Then he began the serious slow business of rolling a smoke.

I went back to the sights. The view was as crisp and coloured as a spring morning; the Fiore's cross-whiskers reached back through my eye to focus my very brain-stem. She had everything but a pulse.

'We don't want to drop 'em right there on the step.' I tried to sound businesslike instead of excited. 'Or no one else'll come out. We want to get 'em along the boulevard, or once they hit the park there.'

Jelly manoeuvred his back up the wall and squinted out the

window-crack. 'Hmmm.' He slid down into his squat again, clinked open a lighter and set the rollie going. His eyes were puffy and bruised like a gangmaster's, and his fingers had tiny shakes. *He didn't make the auditions, this Jelly bloke*, Dogleg had told me. *But that's all I know about him. 'Cept that now, his heart's in the right place. You don't need to worry about that.* 'Some of them'll just hang out there, for a smoke or some Dutch courage. On the step. Gabbing.'

'Yeah, like Red Enjin, and Harry the Lair, and the ones in a troupe, like the Bangers or the Russian guys – they hang about together.'

'We could do them all, last off,' said Jelly. 'Send a rocket in. Blow our cover and be gone.'

'Except how would we know it *was* last off? Say we take out the Bangers – maybe Otto and his Atlantics were about to pop out for a smoke. It'd be a sin to miss them.'

Jelly sucked on the rollie. 'When we feel satisfied.' He tapped his chest. 'That's when we're finished. When we've made a dent in the programme. When there's enough gone to give us a warm fuzzy feeling.'

'If you say.' I didn't often get those, myself. I got colder with every hit. Colder and more steely.

Right on twelve hundred, a little flock of bouffons burst from the door, pulling out puffers and pill-bottles and chequered handkerchees. I startled – they were suddenly so close, I could see the sweat beading through their pancake.

'They're all in a clump, but moving,' I said. 'There's Dugald, and Tiny Robina, and a few amateurs – do we want amateurs?'

'Why not? Hobbies are the pros of the future.' Jelly

35

scratched his scalp energetically. Psoriasis lurked along the hairline, ready to run out and pink-and-white his face any second.

'Well, they're still all togeth— Hang on, they're splitting. Tiny's off by himself. He's in a hurry somewhere.'

'Tiny's a good one to start with. Start off small, eh. Start off tiny. Geddit?' Jelly didn't laugh.

'I will.' I panned after Tiny along the boulevard towards rue Bleu. I knew he'd go up the little alley just before it, because Bleu was bad with the gangs. As soon as he turned in, where his pink and gold silks wouldn't be seen from back down the street, I squeezed. The Fiore *thunked* softly, like a high-class staple gun. Tiny starfished, fell and curled up like a prodded caterpillar. 'He's down.' The relief was a spout of iced water in the middle of my back; I'd wanted a good start.

'Dugald. Ugly mug. Pokes kiddies, too.'

'They all do, if you listen to some people,' I said quickly. I didn't want him to start on *those* stories, thank you. 'There he is, peeing on a tree.'

'Excellent. Get him like that.' Jelly scrambled around to look.

Thunk. In the sights, Dugald arced over backwards, and his pee arced after him. He planted his face in the soft earth and lay still. 'See the backflip?' crowed Jelly. 'Even *I* saw that!'

'So I'll get the hobbies?' I hunted through the sights.

'Naah, I've changed my mind. Let's not waste ammo on 'em. Let's only go for name brands, hey?' He cackled and got out his notebook and pince-nez and push-pencil. 'Ones we know and love,' he added in an acid, upper-crust voice. He'd come a ways, too, only downwards.

Jelly wrote the two names carefully in the book. He had quite a list already. 'How's it looking?'

'Someone in white. Big.'

'Could be Parrot?'

'I thought Parrot was all colours. Um, like a parrot?'

'Not these days. He went *ironic*, didn't he?' I could almost hear Jelly's eyes rolling. 'Set up a *dialogue*, you know? An opposition? Between signifier and signified? Tedious.'

'Well, he's got a green wig.' I sensed there were a lot of rants and raves ready to run out of Jelly and pin back my ears.

'Oh, it won't be him, then.'

'It's written on him . . . Mint Patty.'

'Course. Yeah, brrr. The ukelele man. What a gimmick. Yes, we have no bananas. I've got a luvverly bunch of—'

'And Mista Glista.'

'Blast him out of his sequins.'

'They're going off together, down towards the Palais.'

'Anyone else with 'em?'

'No, the others must be going to Nero's. You rapid-fired with this thing?'

'You bet. No problem for the Cha-cha to take 'em both out.'

But they lined up so neatly I got them in one. 'Will you look at that?' I stepped back so he could check through the sights the puddle of white silks and orange sparklies, dropped neatly round the bend in the boulevard.

'Very nice,' he said smokily.

I quite liked the smoke smell, and I could see what he meant about the feeling when you breathed it. I could take it up myself. But there were too many other things to spend

37

money on right now. The borrow of this weapon, for a start. Tools to improve the world with. Tools for doing good.

'Oh, look, they're flooding out!' Jelly was still at the sights. 'Blackbird, Prince Prawn, the Tumblin' Dice. Wouldn't I like to put a rocket into that lot! Ants 'n' Pants . . . Look, a Flying Orologio Brother! What a colourful band of beloveds. Which one'll I pick off?' He dialled with his cigarette hand, the smoke muddling the air around his fingers. 'Ah, Your Highness. Not a good idea to split off to the pie shop today.' *Thunk*, said the Fiore gently, as if it knew it had to stay secret. 'And Blackety Blackbird, lighting up at the park gate? I don't think so.' *Thunk*. Could I ever be patient enough to save up for a Fiore of my own?

Jelly stood back, coughing. 'Here, you better get those Dice – they're heading Dugald's way. Any old sec they'll turn and run.'

'I'm onto it.'

I caught them in the cross-whiskers just as they stopped and baulked. *Thunk-thunk.*

'And then someone'll see *them*,' grumbled Jelly, 'and someone'll see *that* someone, and before you know it we'll have a trail of 'em leading out into the open and the rest'll go to ground.'

'Yeah, but we'll have got so many.'

'But we won't have *chosen*. We'll just have dropped anyone who happened by.'

I shrugged. 'It's all good deeds.' I didn't care, as long as painted people were falling.

'I guess.' But he sounded unhappy.

I got back to work, as much as I could. Most of the bouffons were gasbagging in groups on the boulevard, though one bunch of smartypantses were in the park swapping juggling secrets. There were just too many, all within sight of each other. 'My mouth's actually watering,' I laughed to Jelly. 'Imagine picking off Miam-Miam! Is it worth risking, d'you reckon?'

'We've got the whole week. Let's not get 'em really worried 'til, say, Thursday. Or they'll all bunker down and we'll sit here on our freezing bums wasting rental money. Who was that last one?' he added, pencil poised.

'Enigma. I popped 'im in the canal.' With my bare eyes I could just make out the ballooned black cross of him, twirling slowly down the silver stormwater. 'So, no more big names today?'

'I'd say.'

The sun came out, just the one patch cruising along the boulevard like a travelling spotlight, picking out the shimmering silks, the fright-wigs, the tinsel-cloaks, the red noses like an outbreak of pox. The buffoons did what you'd expect when the limelight hit them: spread their arms at themselves, kowtowed, cartwheeled and sprouted flowers.

'Aw, *gawd*. It'd make you *sick*.'

'Foul, eh?' Jelly was leafing through his notebook.

'Here come the Yellow Jerseys for the day. With a bottle. They're cracking it.'

'Blow 'em awa-ay,' jeered Jelly. 'Who are they?'

'Dunno— Hang on, it's shaved into their hair. TAT . . . and . . . Tat and Tit?'

'La-amel Take 'em out!'

'I can't. They're in a crowd. Everyone's congratulating them, slopping fizz around.'

'Rocket time! If only. No, maybe Thursday we'll treat ourselves to a little mayhem. But we could pick off the Yellows every day. So by Wednesday they'll know: if they win the Yellow, they're worm-food. They'll go pale under their pancake when they're announced. Ha! Tit and Tat, eh?'

'*Tif*. Tat and Tif.' The names were the only hair the two had, in black on pink. The elastic of their giant white beards dug lines across their shiny pink scalps. 'Frikkin' . . . Santy Clauses or something.'

Jelly hawked and spat. 'Oh, how very à la mode. Cultural referencing. Like, what a contribution to the evolution of clowning. Puke-erama. Blow 'em. I hate 'em. And if they're Yellow, they'll only be trouble later.'

'I never heard of them. They must be just jumped up from hobbies. I seen them before, though. Maybe in a troupe or something.'

'They clear yet?'

'They will be soon. Heading for the park. Swilling drink. Hang on, one of 'em's choking on it.'

'Make him die of that choking fit.'

'If I could make it look natural. But you don't jump two metres sideways in the middle of coughing. He's okay now, anyway. That's it, Tat, give him a good thump on the back. Oh, perfect sound effects, Jell – right in sync.'

'Whassat?' Despite that monstrous gob, Jelly's voice still had major rattles.

'Tif just hoiked and gobbed in perfect time with you. Nearly as much, too.'

'So they're in the park? What are you waiting for?'

'They're in full view of the street.'

'Blow 'em anyway. Let's finish here and get some dinner. Couldn't you go a schnitzel sandwich?'

'They're heading for that little glade, with the fountain. I'll pop 'em there.'

'You better. I've already written 'em down.' He got up and shrugged on his backpack, slapped his pockets.

'Okay, okay, give me a sec.'

I flang Tat over the fountain, tumbled Tif as he fled towards the trees. Then I lovingly dismantled the Fioreschiacciare and its tripod and put them in the case, and we left.

I always hated to stop, to find myself back on some rooftop stacked with age-old rubbish bags, or in some empty office strewn with files, dead clerks' jackets over the backs of all the chairs. Plus the eating and networking part of the game didn't grab me. Although, I'll give you, it was better than *not* eating.

I followed Jelly down the corridor, pushing through the dusty crimson interval-curtains, glimpsing rooms that were hardly trashed at all, the flocked gold paper still on the walls, the corners still fitted with honeywood prie-dieux, which one bad winter would turn into someone's firewood. The troupes had been through just after the torch, defacing the place. Now, instead of the nuns' Holy Man, the biggest bouffon of all, the Weeping Yay-Zou, mawked down on us from frame after curly-gilt frame, his red nose sometimes a plastic blister, sometimes lovingly painted red with a white dot of shine, sometimes a big cabochon ruby, almost worth pinching. Nah, hot rubies didn't fetch as much as they used to – besides, what was I thinking? My thieving days were over; I was on the greener side of the fence now, eh?

We went to the Puffin. It was pricier than the Spectacled

Eider – we were paying for all the mirrors and chandeliers and plaster dolphins on the walls – but the food was better and we reckoned we deserved it. We had good soup and cod, and fine glasses of fizz, toasting our morning's work and the days ahead of us. All around us were the people who keep the world running: riggers and sweepers, ticket-sellers and physiotherapists, with a sprinkling of top hats and tailcoats.

'How about you, then?' said Jelly. 'Dogleg said you were a lone ranger.'

'I'm no party-man.' I toyed with a flake of cod. 'Always wanted to be a Hectic, and do it with a knife, and say something. But I couldn't stomach being so close. Couldn't put on the pancake, even pretending.'

I put down my fork. Jelly saw me do my twitch, which is everything pressed tight, lips and fists and toes in boots, to get the feeling of white-muck off my skin. A twitch like that could come from several kinds of pasts, and he waited, until I could pick up my fork again.

'I got brought up in homes,' I said, starting on the potted version I could tell without too much trouble. 'State ones, not nuns'. The stars, they could walk in after a show and have their pick of us.'

I could read him like a matinee poster. There was some sympathy in his shudder, but his look said, *And they picked you? Pull the other one.*

'I never got properly done over,' I assured him. 'It came close once, that's all.' *That's all you need. You don't need more than that.* 'But other kids did. Every Thursday and Saturday night, for years. All those buffoons, the Grand Old Men of the Ring, they'd be dead now – Barley Charlie and the like.

Jiminy Grinshine. Too late to go whacking them. But all my life the kids they buggered up have been dropping off roofs and throwing themselves under elephants' feet. And you've gotta do something.'

He sipped his fizz. 'Ah, yes. You do, too.' His conviction was there, as intense as mine, though it came from quite some other place. Well, he could keep that place to himself; I wasn't curious.

We were just umming and ahhing between the passionfruit mousse and the chocolate salami when a woman called out, 'Gerald! Darling!' in a true Big Top voice.

Jelly looked past me and wilted. 'It's my mum,' he muttered. 'Act classy.' He put on a weak smile and stood up. 'Mother! You shouldn't come into a place like the Puffin.' Ew, the accent on him.

'Saw you through the *win*-dow!' She kissed Jelly on both cheeks. She was quite a sight in her stage-pancake and tutu and her auburnised croquembouche hair. And she smelled, too – one of the clean, old, bottled scents, magnolia or something. Jelly stood in the cloud of it, very much the shaggy son.

'I just heard, and I had to tell you, darling: Freddy and Felix won the *Blouson d'Or* at the Jeux this morning!'

'The what?' said Jelly.

All eyes in the Puffin were on the mother now. Except Jelly's – he looked at me.

'*You* know,' said his mum. 'The prize! The Yellow Jersey! For the day's best bouffons! Don't be thick, darling. You know what I'm talking about.'

'My brothers,' Jelly said to me. 'Twins. Very talented.'

I tried to show nothing. A dreadful burp of cod and fizz rose in my throat. *Now I know what you'd look like, Jelly, with a big white beard strapped to your face, sans the hair, sans the bags under the eyes. Young. Hopeful. Full of juice and ghastly fun.* Show nothing. Hold still until Jelly shows how much he minds. Then just echo that, on my own face. That's the safest.

'But . . . Hobbies can't win a Blouson,' Jelly said. 'They can't even go in the—'

She tutted and sighed. 'I *told* you they'd been jumped up.'

'You did?'

'Yes, at the Mask Ball, remember?'

'I didn't go,' said Jelly hollowly, lifting his gaze from me to his mum. 'I didn't go to the Mask Ball.'

She stamped her slipper. 'Well, *anyway*. Tit for Tat, they call themselves, and they're *very* good. I mean, clearly! The premier Blouson at their very first games! Isn't it marvellous?'

In my mind's eye, Tat draped himself over the fountain. Even without the bullet, that crack to the head would've— And Tif ran for the trees, his real mouth square with terror. He tripped on his billowing silks, he tumbled like a popped balloon— Nope, there was no going back.

'Marvellous,' Jelly said. 'Will there be a party?'

His stagy curiosity made her face light up. 'Oh, darling, will there! Bring all your friends!' She gave me a three-quarter back view of the croquembouche – she'd be doing something with her face to say, *Not* this *friend, though.*

'I will! I'll be there!' Jelly brayed.

'Tonight!' And she swept out of the Puffin, touching a petit-chou of her hair, her tutu wagging above her jewelled hosiery. All she needed was a white pony and a circle of sawdust to ride around.

The burp came out through my nose – it was soundless but it fouled the magnolia air. Jelly watched me watch him, his face mask after mask, each the tiniest bit different, but the eyes always dark, almost smoking.

'That will be a fun do,' I ventured, when he looked down at the dessert menu.

He winced. 'What can they expect!' he spat.

'It's only fair,' I said evenly. I laid my hand on the Fiore case, thinking of the slow squeeze and *thunk* of firing her, so smooth and leisurely. *And the way it lifts them, all slow-motionly, their silks flapping, the mouth inside the painted mouth opening, the nose drawing a red curve on the sight-screen—*

'Made up your minds, gentlemen?'

I came out of my twitch and blinked at the waiter, standing there with his pencil cocked, kiss-curls painted across his forehead.

'I can recommend the mousse,' he said. 'Light as a feather, but *intense* flavour.'

Jelly dug for money and folded it into the waiter's hand. The man backed off bowing when he felt the quantity. My mouth hungered after passionfruit, but was I going to insist? Jelly picked up the Fiore.

I concentrated hard, following him through the markets, dodging loaf-stalls, iced-bun stands, sproutings of glazed-dough kewpie dolls on candy-sticks. Night was closing in. Was I going to lose him, and the Fiore along with him? Would he go all funny, turn on me? These rich kids, how much could you rely on them?

He led me through the safety fence around the church tower, in through the shot-away door, up the stairs, out onto the balcony-thing. He sat himself between two winged gargoyles with their heads knocked off, and I parked nearby. There was a chilly wind, and the rain was coming on again. Below, the market glittered pink like a rosette-firework, but the rest of the city was a wet freight of stonework, stacked all the way to the horizons. Jelly sat hunched as a gargoyle himself, smoking and coughing and smoking, his rollies sheltered under his hand.

I tried out several sentences in my head. *See, I haven't got brothers* . . . But of course I did. Lobby Boyd, Frik-knuckles Weinstein, Tooley Kochinski – all those kids I grew up with. If they weren't brothers what were they? If they weren't brothers, why was I doing this with my life? *It's all good deeds.* But it wasn't, was it? It was one bad deed piled on another like camp-corpses, like gar-bags in an abandoned bunker . . . *Could I try one of those smokes?* But he might decide to hit me, and I wasn't large, and there wasn't room here for my kind of fighting.

One more coughing fit, one more rollie, and Jelly seemed to come awake – well, in a blind sort of way. He opened the Fiore case and took the baby out, and all her kit, piece by piece. He set her up, as if for the first time and learning as he went. Off to one side, I closed the case so the rain wouldn't ruin her blue crushed-velvet bedding.

Jelly pointed her at the rainclouds through a gap in the stone balusters. I was quite happy to admire her. I could see why he'd – what, console himself? – with the sight of her all solid and beautiful, with the thought of Benato drawing her forth out of nothing, into metal and usefulness. It was enough to look at her, without sullying her with actual work. Jelly was right.

But then.

Jelly brought a foil out of his jacket. He unwrapped it too carelessly for it to be drugs. Worse than drugs, a white nub of something glowed in the gloom. My whole body pulled back from it against the tower wall.

He didn't need a mirror. He drew a perfect white oval around his face from hairline to chin-dimple, and filled it in. The stuff clagged on his eyebrows and stubble; it waxed his fingertips; it brought his every wrinkle and pore into relief. My twitch came on and turned my body to rock.

Next, Jelly produced a red-lead crayon. He drew himself a mouth, as if in his sleep; a million times before, he'd done this. It was as smooth and shiny as a rubber stick-on. As it always does, the lipless, puckery real mouth gave the lie to the big-happy drawn one; if he looked at me, I would wet myself. The old terrors were frothing the fizz I'd had, kicking up the cod. All this time and running I'd spent, and here I was, plastered on the church-stone like a splatted paint-ball, trapped with one of the things hardly an arm's reach away, in full muck—

It got worse. He put the nose on. It made him move differently; it gave him that terrible pretend-childlikeness they have. The face dipped and floated as he stood, *ooh!*, surprised to find himself, *why, here!* A breath honked into me, the first for a while.

He shook his khaki jacket inside out, off his hands, then tweaked it again somehow, so that it burst open into layered orange furbelows. He stepped into it and stretched, becoming the familiar, dreaded star-shape, his feet orange-bootee'd on the pocked stone, his fingers gloved in tight orange kid. A practised *zip* and he was gone, leapt up the ladder to the class he belonged in. He unclipped the backpack; it was brimming with clown-gear, packed special so he could 'discover' it in a certain order.

As soon as he started, I could tell he was good. Why hadn't they taken him at the auditions? He must've choked badly on the day. He juggled as if the knives, the firesticks, the golden coshes weighed nothing, as if they were making their own crescents and circles, with his hands just patting them for reassurance. He tumbled like a squirrel, running up wall and down balustrade, flipping along the stone coping as if nothing yawned beyond, as if the city were a safety net he'd never *think* of needing. He mimed all the mimes: the full three-course meal, the stint in the mini-car, the case-of-mistaken-identity; he slipped from pose to ritual pose through the rolls and shocks and blanches I remembered, in my bones and muscles, from my own classes in the homes – except perfect, never wondering what the point was. Not a fumble, not a wobble, not a pause.

The only thing that saved me was, he didn't once look my way. He played to some other audience. I heard them laugh as he pratfalled and pretended pain; they cried and blew their noses as he sat alone in the sawdust-moted spotlight with the solo fiddle curling its tendrils among the tentpoles; they screamed with love of him when he recovered at the sight of the Pretty Girl and exploded in feathers. I knew that crowd; they'd watched me, too, as I rose and rose; they'd applauded and delighted and shouted, 'Yes!' They weren't real – a crowd like that can only exist in your head. The loudest voices in my crowd, for example, were the dead ones. Which didn't stop me always trying to *show* them, to fix things up with them *once and for all*.

Jelly stood spread-eagled the final time. The hiss of rain on stone was like distant cheers, and he bathed in them. His hair was all bedraggled, but his orange frills were of such stuff that the rain balled up and rolled off him, in sprays like beads wired to his costume.

He must have heard me not clapping, my absence of delight. 'What was your name again?' he said, his face pushed into the light-bruised rainclouds.

If it's got a red nose, never tell it your true name, said Frik-knuckles before he went off to the tram-station to lay his head on the rail. *Or he'll call you it, and call you it, until the sound of it in anyone's mouth will just about make you chunder. Call yourself Billy or Tommy or anything that's not your name. That way it can be happening to that other kid, and you can keep your own name for yourself.*

I peeled my arm off the stonework. It was a travesty of movement after Jelly's act; it wonked and groped towards the Fiore. But, *thunk*, she said anyway – *she* was certain, even if I was wobbly.

Did Jelly spring as well? I don't know how much of that last back-somersault he intended. Or whether he did actually stop a moment, out past the broken lip of the balcony, and catch my eye, through the rain, before he dropped.

The rain hissed. The merry-go-round jingled and groaned below. Slowly my body came out of the twitch. The bouffon would fall in the churchyard mud, inside the safety fence. No one would see him; no one would have seen him go down, if I was lucky.

And I was lucky. I was always lucky. I put the Fiore to bed, and my hands weren't even shaking. Not now, with that thing out of sight.

I stepped over the strewn bunting, the grouped sticks and coshes. I was balanced, even with the case; I could glide its weight down the stairs with my speediest tippy-toeing. All the way down, I took care not to think of that bouffon struggling bloodied round the tower, to meet me at the shot-away door with another spurt of ghastly tumbling.

And of course he didn't. I was lucky.

I ducked through the fence into the markets, the Fiore like a tiny heavy coffin in my arms. No alarms were sounding; nobody was running; nobody paid me any mind at all. I walked through the markets, sober and dark as a shoeblack or an electricity man, as a man carrying his work case, going about his business.

sweet pippit

We set out in the depth of night, having held ourselves still all evening. Hloorobnool was poor at stillness, being only in her fifties. But our minder was a new man; he likely thought she rocked and puffed and raised her trunk like that every sunset. We could all have reared up and trumpeted, no doubt, without alarming that one. But our suffering was close to the surface; better to keep it packed into a tight circle than to risk rampage and shooting by letting it show.

With the man gone to his rest, Booroondoonhooroboom set to work. She used her broken tusk on the gateposts, on the weak places where the hinges had been reset after Gorrlubnu's madness. Pieces pattered to the ground as softly as impala dung. She worked and she sang, drawing the lullaby up around us. Before long we were all swaying in our night-stances, watching Booroondoon with our ears and our foreheads as well as our eyes.

And then she had done loosening.

'Gooroloomboon,' she said, and Gooroloom came forward. The two of them lifted aside the chained-together gates, and there between the gateposts was a marvellous wide space. We had not expected it, somehow – though had we not all said, and planned, and agreed? Ah, it is a difficult thing, the new, and none of us like it much. We swayed and regarded the open gate. We were accustomed at the most to circling these gardens, with an owda on our back full of tickling peeple, and our mahout on our head.

It took Booroondoon, our queen and mother, still singing very low, to move into the space, to show us that bodies such as ours *could* move from home into the dark beyond. And as soon as the darkness threatened to take her, to curtain her from our sight, it became not possible for any of us to stay.

And so we moved, unweighted, from the gardens; Hmoorolubnu took my tail, as if that small thing would hold her steady in this storm of freedom. Zebu groaned at us behind their rails, and a goat on the stone hill lifted its head and gave brittle cry. But our bearing is the sort that soothes others; we move with inevitability, as the stars do, as the moon swells and shrinks upon the sky. We brushed aside the wooden gatehouse as if it were a plaything we had tired of, and the other animals remained calm. Gooroloom tumbled it to sticks, and our feet crushed it to dust. Above the dark and swollen river of our rage, my delight in our badness hung briefly bright.

His name was something like Pippit. It was too short for our ears to catch, as all peeple's names are; twig-snaps and bird-cheeps, they finish before they properly start. But his smell was a lasting thing, and his hand. Pippit of all peeple could tell badness from goodness, as we could. He would know that this was our only choice, he who could still us with a word, whose slender murmuring soothed us when all other voices were pitched too high and madding, who slept fearless among our feet and rode us without spear or switch – whom we missed in a rage of missing, ever since he had been taken from us to somewhere in the dark out-world.

Gooroloomboon spoke through her forehead, wonderingly: 'How our minds have become circle-shaped, from all our circling, squared from pacing that square! Once we were wild! But I fear I have no wildness any more, Booroondoon; maybe wildness has died in my blood and my feet can move *only* in circle and square. What are we to do for water and for food, mother? And how are we to know where to find our sweet Pippit? And if he be in a place that requires badness to reach him, can we do such a thing, even in his name?'

Booroondoon, her graciousness, heard Gooroloom out. 'Put away your fears,' she said, even as she lullabied. 'Fears are for little-hearts, or the lion-hunted. I have never been wild in my life, yet our Pippit's track through this world is as clear as a stripe of water thrown across a dry riverbank. What you love this much, you can always find again.'

And our spirits, which had been poised to sink with Gooroloom's worry, lifted as if Booroondoon's words were buoyant water, as if her song were breeze and we were wafted feathers.

We walked out among peeple's houses, that were like friends standing beside the path. With every sleeping house we passed, I was more wakeful; with every step I took that was not circle-path, or earth we had trodden as many times as there are stars, something else broke open in me. My mind seemed a great wonderland, largely unexplored, my body a vast possibility of movements, in any direction, all new.

There would be food and water, good and bad – Gooroloom would smell them, too, when she finished fretting. I wanted to lift my head and trumpet, but there was joy also in knowing I must not, in moving with my fellows through the sleeping town, making no sound but planting feet and rubbing skin and the breath of walking free.

We came to the town's edge. Without pausing, Booroondoon continued on under the moon towards nothing, only parasol trees that cannot be eaten, only a line that had stars above it, dry shadows below. We followed, and the town smells fell behind. Hloorobn, ahead of me, lifted her trunk. I head-bunted her rump, to keep her quiet, and she grunted low in surprise. Then we settled to a strong pace after Booroondoon, rolling our yearning rage out onto the plain.

Several hours on, we were suddenly among the bones. Heightened as our senses were, we'd not anticipated these. And it is always difficult to move on from such places. Hloorobn, in particular, hung by the remains of her mother, our sister, Gorrlubnu, lifting and turning the bones, urging us to take and turn them also, tipping the great headbone with a thud and a puff of moon-silvered dust.

Booroondoon went among the bones telling the names once only, touching the heads and leaving us to turn the lesser bones. Then she waited beyond, facing our goal but in all other respects patient, allowing us our youth and rawness and powerful pain, though her own was long ago distilled into wisdom and grace.

We went on, our thoughts like weighted owdas slowing our steps.

We walked far that night. Booroondoon said we should go

56

straight out, for an improbable distance that peeple would not follow.

'And if they do?' said jittery Hloorobn. 'If they surprise us?'

'What can they do against so many Large?' said Booroondoon. 'Cannot herd if we will not listen. Can try, with their spear, but will have to spear us all to stop us.'

She meant that such a spearing was not likely. But then, their taking Pippit had not been likely, either, yet it happened. In this night of walking in the wild, nothing was certain as it used to be.

Towards dawn, we found water. There was no town behind us, no town ahead, only grassed plain, and rounded rocks like friends browsing. When we had drunk, we moved straight on, slower for a while to try the wild grass, pulled up sweet and still living. Booroondoon sang no longer, for we did not need to be led by that means now; we had seen our own courage and were rallied and moved and unstoppable.

So the day passed, and several others like it. There was a night and day of terrible thirst, born of the need to walk a straight line from our starting point. Then we came to a broad, clear river, and we swam it, and stood in the shallows on the far side, and the water was magnificent in our throats, a delight across our backs.

Late that day, when we had satisfied our thirst and settled the fears arising from it, Booroondoon said, 'The place we want is not far now.'

We sensed it, a big, rubbishy restlessness far down-river, a swarming movement in the ground that made our feet unhappy.

'We must go into the midst of that?' said Gooroloom.

'They will not bring him out to us,' said our wise mother.
We walked awhile on the thought.

Then, 'I have it,' said Booroondoon. 'We will walk into the
town as if we were led, so as to calm the little-hearts. We will
go in a line, trunk to tail, and with care where the way is
narrow. We must move slowly, for our Pippit's smell may be
easily lost among all the others, markets and meateries and
skinworks and the like. But if we go graciously and let neither
dogs nor peeple fright us – do you hear me, Hloorobn? – if we
stay together in our line, we cannot be thwarted.'

'As you say, mother and queen,' we replied.

We decided we would go into the town just before day
hurried out of night, when the smells and peeple-movements
would be less. Until that hour we lurked at a distance, in a
bad place – stenchful, with death-birds crowding sky and
ground.

Their headwoman flapped to the top of the rubbish nearest
us. 'Any of youse sick?' she skrarkled, eyeing us all.

Hloorobn rumbled too low for her to hear.

'Anyone dropping a baby soon? Youse all look pretty big,'
said the bird hopefully.

Booroondoon swung up her trunk, and the bird staggered
away: 'Just asking, just asking!'

'Disgusting,' said Hloorobn.

'Shudderable,' Gooroloom agreed.

'Take no notice,' said Booroondoon. 'We are Larger.'

There was nothing to eat in this place, so we began, in the
night, to feel wretched, all bulk and no bone, our minds
spinning like the moon on its wheel.

'If only he were here,' said Gooroloom, 'if only we already

58

had him! This venture frightens me, now it is near to finishing.'

It was good that she spoke, or my own fears would have bubbled up into my forehead and made themselves known. I could not keep Gorrlubnu out of my head, how after months of uncanny stillness, where Pippit soothed and Booroondoon leant and all of us huddled around her, she had slipped her mind as your foot slips a loose tether-loop, and gone crashing from our lives; how she burst the gates with her head and bent them underfoot; how, unthinkably, she left Booroondoon's commands ignored upon the air. We stood voiceless and mindless, as peeple leaped and twinkled after her. At Booroondoon's knee, tiny Pippit jolted as Gorrlubnu struck about her; he cried out when she roared. She swam away through the market. Fruits sagged out of their pyramids and broke on the ground; chicken cages tumbled and sprayed feathers.

The marketers came to the gate-opening, yabbering and shaking their fists at Pippit, but we had ears only for the receding commotion of our sister, Gorrlubnu, the drumbeat of her madness, and the lesser impacts and explosions around it. Until a single blunderbuss shot saved her from worse rampage, bringing all other sounds to stillness, so that across the town, through all its wreckage and outrage, we heard clearly the thunder-crash that was Gorrlubnu striking the ground; her lips shuddering on the breath thus crushed from her; the dry scrape of her feet dying in the dust.

She has found the Forest Hills of legend, breathed Booroondoonhooroboom, our queen. *She is pressing her forehead against the first browsing-tree.*

Only singing brought us through that hungry night amongst the refuse, a tether of rumbling song through the slowest part of the sun's race round. Whenever my thoughts made me fall quiet, the singing strengthened into my hearing, and drew me in again.

'Very well,' said Booroondoon in the deepest hour. We all heard her; none of us were asleep.

We walked a nightmare road. The cold breeze blew peeple-rubbish and rattled rotten paper. Would we lose our nose for Pippit, amongst all this ordure? Booroondoon moved ever queenly ahead.

The town began gradually, with rubbish-pickers' shelters, the children sleeping as if thrown down, bare on the bare ground. Then wood-walled houses sidled up to the road, which widened and hardened, and finally, along the cleanest avenues, brick and stone palaces rose higher than ourselves, textured with carvings. And after days of golden grass, and trees nearly black in their thirst, here were green vines and hanging plants spilling over the palace walls, their flowers set like jewels among their bright, water-fat leaves.

We came to a circle that seemed purpose-made for owda rides, within a ring of empty stalls. There we joined trunk to tail and became still, to listen and breathe, to arrive at the knowledge we needed.

And there Booroondoon said to us, at her lowest, at her farthest from peeple's hearing, 'He is close, very close.' She listened further, then spoke softer, no more than a gentle buzzing in our heads. 'And in sore distress.'

We took pains not to give voice, but anyone who knew us would have heard the trouble in our breathing, the creak of the strong will restraining our movement. Our rage squirmed and whimpered like a creature pinned underfoot, that must be kept from flight, but not be harmed.

'We could break down the place,' rumbled Hloorobn.

'Hush!' we said.

'It would crush Pippit within,' Gooroloom remonstrated.

'We could tear off the doors,' Hloorobn whispered.

'But remember those peeple that took him,' I said, 'with their bright spears. How quick to anger they were! He had real fear of them, so we should, too.'

'There is a terrible smell on him,' said Booroondoon. She tilted her head a certain way, and some of us dropped tail from trunk, and Hloorobn even shifted one foot that way, for the smell was among us for a moment, a flash of fear-sweat, a shaft of some worse thing.

'We know that smell,' said Hmoorolubnu. Booroondoon grunted and twitched her head. All around, trunk rasped on flank, seeking and giving help. 'Our sister Gorrlubnu, remember?'

'No one has forgotten Gorrlubnu,' I hissed, from one of those moments when my tusks gleamed before my eyes, and my whole self seemed funnelled into them.

Others were at my sides, leaning.

'Do you mean Pippit is mad?' asked Gooroloom of the queen, and lifted her trunk and sniffed carefully.

'Is dying,' said Booroondoon. 'Is moving towards death, sure as winter follows summer.'

'He is ill? He is beaten?' I said out of the deep woe that was like mud grasping us, sinking us down to death ourselves. I could not breathe to draw in the scent of him, my trouble was so great.

'Neither of those. He seems whole in body and strength. Only, that smell—' And again it was there, making me want to rear and run. 'I cannot puzzle it.'

'Can we find him?' I said in quiet agony. 'Is it safe to seek him?'

'Let us go and see,' said Booroondoon. She must have known we were about to break bond and rush in all directions. She knew well that it is better to give a little, early on, than to lose all at the last.

We took our places and went in line through trade streets that smelled of paint and spices, shaved metal and wood. Booroondoon brought us among palaces, grimed and weary-feeling. Low in a brick wall there, she found a hole, barred like the one in our night-house. From this one poured the cold stinks of fear, some of them stale when our mothers' mothers were birthed, and some fresh as just-pulled plains-grass, full of juice and colour.

Among them was Pippit's fear – even I could smell it. 'Little man, little man!' I heard myself croon, 'Day's light, night's peace, to what have they brought you?' And we were all around the barred hole, our feet puddling in the fears, and we all spoke, mostly only in our heads, but some in our throats where peeple might hear us, danger or no, we were so pained and grieved.

Then, wonder of wonders, from within the hole came a tiny voice that we knew, calling our names, those chips of bird-cheep he gave us. And we could not help but answer, in our woe.

Gooroloom fluttered a breath into the hole, and there was an immediate ruckus of many peeple in there. Hloorobn grasped one of the window-bars and plucked it out like a twig, and all the peeple inside went silent. She plucked out the other bars, laying them neatly as she had once laid cut logs in her forest work.

And as she pulled the last, peeple boiled out like ants, terrified peeple climbing over Gooroloom's trunk, crawling among our legs, smelling all of filth and illness, but none of them was Pippit. And when they had finished boiling, still Pippit was weeping and calling us from within.

'What is it?' said Hloorobn. 'Have they broken some part of him?'

We drew in our breath at the thought.

'I told you, he is whole,' said Booroondoon. 'But he is deep inside this place. Perhaps there are more bars, between us and him; perhaps he is behind a gate too strong for peeple to breach.'

'But *we* could breach it—'

'Try, Hloorobn!' I urged. 'Get down on your knees and reach in!'

She did so, while we all whispered help and surance, past her head, to Pippit inside.

'There is nothing,' Hloorobn rumbled in disgust. 'Nothing but roof and air as far as I can reach. And there is no light. I can hear no chain – can you? – but their leg-tether may be of rope.'

'Do peeple leg-tether *each other*?' I asked astounded.

'What else would keep him from us? Listen to him, poor nubbet – if he could be with us, he would.' And indeed, I was

63

fighting to listen to Hloorobn and not let my heart be stretched to breaking by the sound of Pippit's weeping.

We murmured to him, and he called to us, until we were all nearly mad with not seeing him, with not taking him up and placing him as a crown on our heads, with not feeling the pat of his little paws on our faces, or the trill of his song, almost too high for us to hear, as he plied the soapy hard-broom on all our backs in turn. What joy we had had, commanded by a Pippit, who knew no fear of us but only love, who cared for us so closely and so well – it was hard to remember that he was not a Large like one of us, and could not hear our loving head-talk.

'We must go,' wept Booroondoon at last. 'Dawn rushes towards us. We cannot reach him, and it will do him no good to hear us being speared out here.'

'They would never,' said Gooroloom. 'They only spear mad ones, like Gorrl—'

'We must go. Somewhere we can think, where we are not flayed by our beloved's sadness. If we stay here, we will fall to mindlessness with our pain, and do him no good.'

And so, suffering and weeping, we drew away.

'Will he know we intend to come back?' worried Hloorobn.

'The child is so close to death, we are no more than a dream to him,' soothed Gooroloom.

'And perhaps we can be no more than that comforting dream,' said Booroondoon. 'Perhaps we must be content with that.'

By some route I did not see, through a daze of mourning, Booroondoon led us to a cleared part of town. The smell of dead ashes lingered in the place, so a fire must have brought the structures down, but now all the rubble was gone, and the soil beneath was combed flat.

We tried to gather ourselves, but could do little more than sweep our woe back and forth. Was our only choice to turn and follow our own tracks home, and live out our long lives under fearful spike-men, stung by their beatings, nagged by their needling voices?

'I would rather seek the Forest Hills,' said Gooroloom. 'What is a life without Pippit?' And we mourned and sighed around her.

'Come, we must put our minds to this,' said Booroondoon. 'We must stand in a line as if we were peeple-bid, and let schemes brew in our heads.'

But no sooner had we arranged ourselves than the town began to stir around us.

'What is this?' said Hloorobn. 'Peeple never rise so early.'

'Not in such numbers,' said Gooroloom. 'Only marketers and street-sweepers come out before dawn.'

'I do not like the feeling of it,' said Booroondoon.

As soon as she said it, my bones felt a deep unease, as if they could slip unset somehow, as if we might fall to pieces inside our skins. 'Nor I,' I whispered.

Even before the first few muffled peeple passed us, all walking the same way, we could feel that the town's quiet activity was bent like spring grass under a steady wind, an eagerness like river-water pulling. But instead of the sweetness of water, instead of the scents of bud and pollen and new leaf, this pulling breeze carried a low stink, a tang of chain-metal, a sour-sweet dreadfulness.

We stood close together as dawn came on, trying to find

some other scent on the air to disperse the stink. 'I wish we were home again,' whispered Hloorobn. 'Around this time, he would be stirring awake in the straw, our little man . . . Do you remember when he first saw us, how the child ran to Booroondoon and flung his tiny arms about her leg?'

'We must go,' said Booroondoon, 'for he sleeps not on straw but on stone, and someone is kicking him awake even as we try for courage among our memories.' And she took a step after the passing peeple.

We joined on behind her, some silent, some wittering ('To that death-place?' 'Oh please, my queen!'). We moved after her, deeply against our will, in our orderly line, through the main town. The peeple in flood around us were too intent upon the dreadfulness to realise we went uncommanded. They flowed past full of fear and excitement and relief, their faces always towards their destination.

The place was crowded, with an itch in the air; it was the stuff of bad dreams, to have to pick one's way among such close-packed flimsies. But the platform at the centre, sweet with fresh-sawn wood, was empty, except for two men holding rattle-guns, which smelt not of death but of pride and show. What stank was the blade lying like a moon-sliver on the dark, raised box before them. Through all the crowd there was a craning and a yearning towards this weapon.

Peeple had brought food baskets, seating, children. As day brightened further, parasols began to open and twirl throughout the crowd. A man close by was selling burnt-sugar. One boy carried a small white rat on his shoulder.

'What breed of wrong-hearted festival is this?' I asked it.

'I don't know, but the food is good.'

The crowd was such that we could only form a line, Booroondoon by the platform and the rest of us sheltering behind her from the full force of the blade's stink. She rumbled a message: *Hold Hloorobn,* and I renewed my grasp on Hloorobn's tail. We were trained to be serene among peeple; their chatter stirred habitual serenity from our bones. But they were not our peeple, and this was not our town, and we were hungry and thirsty and afraid.

A macao-bird shrieked from the far side of the square: 'Here comes the fun-man, to start off the fun!'

Up the wooden steps climbed a much-bedizened person, with a head-plume, and sparkles on his shoulders. He stood tall between the two guards and spread his arms. The crowd quieted, and the plume-man spoke, his high voice carrying to all corners and every crowded balcony of the square. As he spoke, the peeple grew quieter, and their tides of feeling changed from puzzlement, to disappointment, and finally to alarm and unsettlement.

The macao gave an idiot laugh. 'No whippings today, folk! The monkeys have got out of their cage! The monkeys are running all over town, teasing the watchdogs and busting out the pantries!' Peeple began to pack away belongings, and to edge away from the platform through the crowd. The plume-man made a staying motion with his hands, and kept on speaking, but peeple leaked away, until there were perhaps only half their number remaining. Now we could all move up alongside Booroondoon, and Gooroloom and I could press the excitable Hloorobn between us, flank to flank, and hold her steady.

'Here comes the chopper!' shrieked the macao with glee. 'And the choppee! Say goodbye to your head, bad monkey!'

'There,' said Booroondoon. 'At the great door.'

Raising my head above Hloorobn's I saw a little one, all filthy, being stumbled towards us by two men, also in the sparkling uniforms. Peeple spat on him and squeaked at him as he came. An eddy of breeze brought us his dirt and distress, his being undone by fear, but beneath all that, the familiar, fresh-straw smell of our mahout.

They pushed him up onto the wooden place; they thrust him to his knees there. And someone else had arrived. His close-suit, entirely blue-black, was like a slice of starless night. It covered his face, and stank. Peeple always move too quickly, but this happened in the taking of a single breath. No sooner had we seen him than the blue-black man was making the light flash from the blade, into all parts of the crowd. We were a row of confusions, locked in our mass, as self-less as boulders of the plain.

Then our little ragged one, our Pippit, lifted his head. His hair like dirty ribbons fell back from his face, and he saw us through his staring tear-filled eyes, and knew us.

His knowledge clanked closed upon us like the most welcome leg-iron. His mouth moved on the beloved sound of his command. All of us – in a vast sudden relief at having someone to obey, after our weeks of being chivvied by frightened peeple with sticks, after our days of wandering in the wilderness – all of us lowered our haunches and hoisted our heads and forelegs, to stand giant, to show our true height.

The peeple cleared around us like dust from a sharp blow of breath. Pippit commanded again, and I spoke back as he told me, as did my sisters and our mother our queen. The peeple ran farther away. We spoke with our entire hearts and our full bulk, and every arch and column shook with the noise.

Pippit's voice singled out Booroondoon. The rest of us stood giant, proclaiming our hugeness, trumpeting our obedience and our love.

Their eyes were all in a row, says Booroondoon now, *like children peeping over our garden wall, the men's who held him. The blade-man, he saw me coming; he knew what Pippit was commanding. It happened all so fast – he lifted his sword – he leaped, he was upon Pippit! – and what could I do?*

Nothing but what you did, we reassure her – although, when we saw her fling that blue-black rag out among the peeple, we knew it was a terrible thing she had been driven to.

And then I could just push the others away. Them I did not injure, those ones, did I? They stepped back quietly; they had no swords, you see, and they had seen what I did to the first – so in hurting one I saved at least two—

Also, you had him—

'I have him!' she rumbled to us, and Pippit called us in his bird-voice, even as she swung him onto her head. We moved towards our accustomed order. But seeing Pippit so small and unprotected at our head, and knowing the peeple wished him dead, I pushed forward to precede Booroondoon, as I would have for no other reason, and others came up to shelter him from peeple who might leap up from the sides. Out of the square we went, while the peeple foamed and cried and parted to let us through, and fell back farther as we left the paved part of the town, as we left the housed part, until there were only a few wide-eyed rubbish-pickers' tinies by the road to watch us pass, with our prize on our head, our live, sweet Pippit, chattering and laughing and greeting us by our bird-names over and over.

Which is how we come to be here, on this long walk away from all we know. Since we left the road and the land began undulating, 'Our Pippit may be leading us to the Forest Hills of legend,' Hloorobn says eagerly.

Booroondoon in her sadder moments says, 'He may indeed be leading us into death, for I have never been this way before.'

'And you have been near everywhere there is to be, our queen,' says Gooroloom, 'from the log-camp mountains, to the ports, to the road-making settlements all up and down.'

Says Booroondoon, 'Yet I know nothing of this place, not its rocks or its creatures, nor how Pippit chooses the way among ten hundred sandhills all the same.'

'Who knows? Who minds?' says Hloorobn happily.

'None of us, that's sure,' says Gooroloom.

And none of us does. For each evening our sweet Pippit brings us to water and good browsing, and each morning we wake to a spray of his hot little voice, to the blessing of his kisses and his touch as he walks among us. And he lifts us without spike and leads us without wrath. Singing, always singing, he moves us onward, into each brightening day.

house of the many

Dot was very young. He was in the Bard's house, asking about things, watching his manners.

'This?' said the Bard, taking it down from his shelf. 'This is the House of the Three, isn't it?'

'Yes, Bard Jo.' Dot sat himself to listen.

The Bard sat, too, placing the worn brown box on the mat between them.

'Can you tell me the names of the Three, boy?'

'Anneh, Robbreh and Viljastramaratan.'

The Bard nodded, and Dot glowed inside. 'Anneh, she's the one who wears the pants. She chops all the wood, she hoes the fields, picks the greens and cooks, and leads the animals around. We don't know how she fits all that into her days, but she does, and all the time she's humming and thrumming.'

Dot saw the women bent to the vegetable fields, saw his mother's hands, fine and strong and always busy.

'Robbreh, he's a typical man,' said the Bard. 'He wears the comfortable robes, and he spends all his time in the tea-tent talking wisdom with the Bard. He's happy with very little, as

73

everyone should be. His voice is like a heartbeat. It's so low, it's hard to hear, but it's there all the time.' He raised his gaze from the House of the Three to Dot's face, and nodded reassuringly.

'And Viljastramaratan?' said Dot politely.

The Bard rolled his eyes and made a bitter laugh in his throat. 'Viljastramaratan? That one's a mystery child. Viljastramaratan is not boy and is not girl, or is boy and girl together. Very high, like a mosquito, and distracting like that, and unrestful. Viljastramaratan is always bothering the other two to come and dance. They never do, of course; they just go about their ways and ignore him. So Viljastramaratan weaves song-stuff around them, crazier and crazier, finishing every time in a giggling heap. And when that's quieted, we can hear Anneh and Robbreh again, steady in their song.'

Dot had already heard the Three singing, of course, in snatches of breeze as he lay, sleepless nights, under the starry eye of his house's smoke-hole. But he would not meet them properly until he got to his middlehood, and was allowed to stay up later in the tea-tent. Till then, he was only to hear them accidentally: Anneh thrumming, Robbreh pulsing, Viljastramaratan in wild play around them.

The House of the Three was brown and fragile, like those dead people the wind sometimes uncovered, whose flesh when touched would turn to fine dust, blowing off the browned bones.

'They only come out in autumn and spring, those Three,' said the Bard, 'when the air is damp and right for them. In the dry cold or the dry heat, they're scared to dance and sing.'

'I'm not surprised,' said Dot. 'They would break their own House.'

'It takes Bard Jo and his gentle hands to coax them,' said the Bard. His dark eyes were two points of safety; all sense came from them. 'Only the Bard knows their House, and the corners where they like to hide. And the keys.' Bard Jo's white beard was trimmed short to show his strong chin; he touched one, then the other, of the box's two yellow teeth with fingers kept neat by a wife.

Dot didn't know his father Morri, but he must have been a little taller, a little darker, than anyone else Dot knew. Dot's mother, Bonnch, had taken a vow at Morri's death, and would not offer the Bard any more children than the ones she brought with her, Dot and his sister Ardent. How Dot's mother had attached herself to the Bard's people, no one Dot knew could tell him, but she stayed by being everywhere, by doing everything, tending the plants and animals all through the daylight, working up thread and cloth deep into every night.

'Everybody tells of when they first met the Bard,' said Dot to his mother.

She went on grinding grain. Flicked a glance at him. 'Oh, you want my story?'

'Well, people ask me.'

She ground a little more. 'It's not a story. I came out here and found him after Morri died. I wasn't part of the big move away, right at the beginning. I came later, when my life had readied me for existence in the Bard's ways.'

Dot waited for more. 'Go on.'

She glanced up. 'Go on what?'

'They all say more than *that*. Like what happened when their mums first saw him.'

Her eyes smiled. 'How many of these kids has the Bard as their father?'

'Not all,' defended Dot.

''Cause it's a love story for those ones. Mine is just a deal I did, like a merchant. Not a matter of the heart. It was a way to keep you and Ardent alive, in peace.'

'Did you pay?' said Dot, feeling sinful. He wasn't supposed to be curious about money – none of the Bard's people were.

'I paid all we had, and all Morri had, and all Morri's brother Temba had, who died in the same skirmish.'

'Was that a lot?' whispered Dot, feeling a little sick.

Bonneh went back to grinding, one eyebrow raised. 'I suppose,' she said carelessly. He knew she was hoping he would let it lie, but when she next looked up he was still there waiting.

'Well, my peach . . . on one side there was the money, and Morri's . . . associates, bothering for it all the time. On the other side? Some distance, safety, my two babies, and being left alone. You know I hardly saw your babyhood, with the maids? You remember?'

Dot shook his head. He couldn't remember a time when he hadn't been able to find her anywhere, and watch her hands in their work.

'My father was a merchant, wasn't he? Did you learn from him to make deals?'

'My whole family were merchants and dealers. Like the

Bard says, we were the core of the world's troubles.' She flashed him another smile. 'We fuelled all the evil.'

'But you *repudiated* that,' said Dot, also bringing out some Bard-speak, but earnestly.

'Well, I put it aside, let's say. I was very bitter, after what happened to Morri.' She pointed with her chin. 'Move your sister now. That sunlight is starting to bother her.'

Dot went to the other end of Ardent and pulled the cloth she lay on until her face was in shadow again. That word *skirmish* – for a long time Dot had thought it was some kind of party, with cakes and other immoral things.

His friend Winsome tried not to laugh the day he mentioned that. 'No, it's a war thing,' she said. 'Like a tiny bit of war. Just a quick guns-going-off and then everyone runs away. Except, of course, the ones that gets killed.'

'But guns go off at parties.' Dot was momentarily confused; he'd had the cakes-and-colours picture in his mind for so long. 'People shoot them in the air. I thought maybe the thing bounced off a ceiling or a wall and hit him. The bullet.'

Winsome shook her head. She had the kindest look on her face. 'Out on a road somewhere, it would have been,' she said. 'The truck goes past, and the men with the guns fire from behind a rock, or a building or something.'

Dot had looked down through the Free-Stones game they'd been playing, making over his memory with this new information.

'Something like that,' said Winsome. She was anxious for him.

He gave a sage, Bard-like nod. 'It's your throw,' he said, to move them both on from their embarrassment.

*

Dot's sister, Ardent, had got spoiled somehow, and never grew properly. She was even darker than Dot and Bonneh, and she was all elbows and knees. She was like a folding chair that was stuck halfway between open and closed. She could move her right arm a little; if you put things in that hand, she would appear to play with them. Her left elbow poked straight out in front; that hand was a claw at her right ear. Her eyes looked outward in different directions, and sometimes only one, sometimes neither, was able to fix on things.

Ardent could lie on her left side only, or be carried around in a bag. Bonneh carried her on her back most of the time while she worked during the daylight, or put her under a shade tree nearby. Ardent had to hear voices all the time; her mother's was best, but Dot's would do at a pinch. If you were going to be quiet, you had to let Ardent know you were still there, lean against her or put your hand on her pointed foot, or she would start to jerk and stress.

'My mother sings Anneh,' said Dot, as the Bard got up and lifted the House back to its shelf. 'A lot of the mothers do.'

'And the fathers sing Robbreh,' said the Bard with satisfaction.

'Sometimes the mothers go as low as that, too,' said Dot. 'Or they beat an empty gathering-barrel, which makes something like that sound.'

The Bard frowned down at him.

'It's a better sound,' explained Dot, 'the two voices together.'

The Bard thought for a moment. 'That's true, Dot. For the one cannot live without the other.'

Dot was very young at this time; he couldn't imagine his mother not living, entirely capably, should everyone else except himself and Ardent be taken away by storm or disease or war. But you didn't argue with the Bard.

'No one sings Viljastramaratan, though,' said Dot.

'Pah,' said the Bard, swishing his robes and sitting down again. 'Who would want to? Who would need to? The song of Viljastramaratan is around us all the time, in the racket of the birds and the goats' complaining and all the carryings-on of the children as they play their childish games, or fall and hurt themselves. This song gives men the headache, and must be kept well away. The children, they will learn, when they reach their middlehood, to still their voices to Anneh's or Robbreh's song; as for the goats and the birds, and the myriad other voices of the world, we can do nothing more to calm those than hum Anneh, and throb Robbreh, loud enough to cover them.'

The men went away to town every now and then, when they had to fetch certain things such as medicines, or firewood, or for some relative's funeral. Winsome had heard stories from her dad, about the little plastic house they stayed in, about the coffee-palace where they saw television, which was a box full of alarming music, and moon-faced people kissing each other, and sometimes the soccer. They took two days about it and came back tired and silent, the Bard always very angry until he had swum in his river, and all his children and wives had embraced him.

*

'You never speak to the Bard yourself,' said Dot.

'Don't you worry.' Bonneh was oiling Ardent, who otherwise grew dusty-looking, and twitched and moaned. 'The Bard has plenty of people to talk to him.' She paused to rub the oil in between Ardent's clamped toes. 'He doesn't need my wisdom.'

'And he never talks to you. Except when you're in a bunch and he's talking to everyone, telling them how much to put aside for market or something. He never says anything straight to you, does he?'

'What would he say, boy?' She smiled and swung into longer strokes up Ardent's calves.

'Like he talks to Winsome's mum. Just about children, and work. Then maybe other people would talk to you, too.'

'Darling-darling,' she said with a sigh. 'I had enough of talking, with your father and our families. Nowadays I haven't the patience for people; I work and I watch. I keep this house quiet, for Ardent, and for you to come back to when you want peace. For talk, you can always go to Winsome's house, or Toad's, and soon you'll be middling and visit the tea-tent, too.'

'I'm not worried about me,' said Dot. 'It's you. If the Bard would only act differently – be more friendly.'

'Kids been taunting you about this?'

'No. I've just seen it myself.'

'Hmm. You want to watch those sharp eyes; you might hurt yourself on them.'

There was a boy who must never have slept, and whose ears must have been especially strong to know the Three so well before his middlehood. Down at the river with the water to hide his voice he would *hum* Anneh, and *b'dum* Robbreh, on and on as he built jeeps and rocket-ships out of the mud. Then one day, when spring was on the way and they were all excited for the coming plenty, this boy threw back his head and sang . . . nobody knew who, but if Viljastramaratan had had four sisters and five brothers, dancing together, they might have brought these sounds out. Up shot his voice, as if by accident, wandering among the clouds and jumping from water-point to water-point across the river. Viljastramaratan's baby-coughs and wheezes interrupted the slippery song and gave the boy breath to pour out more.

Dot and all the kids at first laughed. Then as this boy went on, the sounds fountaining out of his mouth so surely, they fell silent. World upon world opened at their ears, worlds of lawless noise and play.

The boy's mother came running, shouting. She knocked him into the mud, waking him up from his singing. They looked at each other, both seeming very frightened. The door of Bard Jo's house moved aside, and the circle of his beard was like a white eye in the shadow. He came out of the house; the way he walked, all the kids shrank together.

The mother stood at her son's muddy head. 'He should not make such a noise,' she said to Bard Jo. 'I'll make sure he's well beaten.' She made herself sound angry to cover up fear.

Bard Jo looked from one to the other, his face all gathered in except the jutting beard. 'I will beat him myself.'

'I won't sing again!' cried the boy. 'Forgive me, Bard Jo!'

'He didn't know what he was doing!' wept the mother. By now she had one of the boy's arms and Bard Jo the other, and the boy was like some grotesque stick doll pulled back and forth over the mud, and muddying the Bard's white dress with his kicking. Dot didn't even know what to be afraid of, but he was sick with it, still as a ghost. Winsome gripped his arm hard.

Bard Jo won the tug of war, being truly angry, while the mother was merely afraid. He got the boy, and the mother stood on the bank, her legs caked to the trouser-rolls in mud, her hands muddying her cheeks as she watched her boy dragged away. He screamed as he went; he quite lost himself, as does a much younger child. He was taken into Bard Jo's house and beaten there, and Dot and the kids sat in the mud and listened to the terrible wordless sounds of Bard Jo's rage, and of the beating, and of the boy. The boy's mother bent and swayed, holding her head, grinding her eyes.

After too long – 'He is killing him!' Winsome whispered – Bard Jo threw the boy out of the house onto his stripes. Mothers came running and took him quickly to his own house, but still there remained on Dot's memory – on the memories of all those kids so that they could never talk about it – the back of that boy, furrowed and weeping like a scored peach from shoulders to thighs, beige dirt patching the slime of it, and the piece – whether dirt or boy they didn't know – that fell from him as the mothers gathered him up.

That boy had always been strange and not talked much, but after that day no one heard a sound out of him. He hardly came out of his house, and even when his back had healed over, he moved all bent and carefully as if the cuts were still fresh.

Dot stayed a favourite of Bard Jo's. He didn't know why.

He feared it was some kind of terrible trick the Bard was planning, to calm and please everyone until the time came for Dot's beating, so that the beating would be a more shocking and frightening thing. Dot could see no reason why he should be favoured above Winsome, whose mother worked so hard and whose father spread the Bard's wisdom every time he opened his mouth. Or above Fanty and Toad and all those cousins, who were like a lot of little Bards running around.

'What about when you first saw my dad, then? Was that special?'

'No.' Bonneh laughed. 'We were children and I hated him. He was one of those Simpsim boys. They were noisy and thought too much of themselves. I hated the lot of them.'

'So how did you get round to marrying one of them?'

'Well, I looked at Morri again, didn't I? With new eyes.'

'And your heart turned over?'

'No, no. I just knew. Our parents were bringing us together, and I knew that it would work all right. He had ears, you see.'

Dot laughed. 'As no one else did?'

'He knew how to use them. He was a very careful man – until all that warring nonsense caught him up. You can hear too much, you know. You can think yourself able to do more about things than you really can.'

'Don't tell me *lessons*,' sulked Dot. 'Tell me about *him*.'

She laughed and went on sorting beans.

On Dot's twelfth birthday, his mother put new white robes on them both and took him to the Bard's house.

'That's a fine boy, Bonneh,' said Winsome's mother as they

passed. Dot's mother had Ardent on her back. Girls didn't have a middlehood; but if they had, Ardent wouldn't have got it anyway. Ardent wasn't going anywhere.

When he came out his door, the Bard looked startled at Bonneh, then up and down Dot as if the boy were an entirely new kind of creature.

'My boy is twelve today and ready to move between child and man,' said Dot's mother.

The Bard recovered himself. 'Twelve already! From a babe in arms, as I remember him.' He looked Dot over as you would judge a skinny sheep that had wandered into camp out of drought. Dot hadn't been at all sure about this. He said nothing, looking at the Bard's neat feet.

The Bard reached forward and pinched his shoulder to make him look up. 'Well,' he said. 'We go to market to-morrow, but Dot may sit with us tonight, to listen and learn.'

Bonneh touched Dot in the small of the back. 'Thank you, Bard Jo,' he said, and looked down again.

They went back to their house and took off the robes. Dot's mother made grilled bean-pats for breakfast while Dot sat against Ardent, feeling miserable.

Bonneh put the platter in his lap and kissed him. 'Don't want to be a man, Dot?' She sat to her own pats and smiled her eyes at him.

'If I were a girl, I could come and work with you.'

'Aah. You always can, anyway, if you want. You're a little different. He won't be hard on you like his own children.'

Dot pushed some bean between Ardent's teeth and didn't answer.

*

When Dot entered the tea-tent that night, the Bard's older sons looked at him as he had known they would.

'How is Dot here?' some said.

'He turned twelve.'

'As I said,' said Pedder, 'how is Dot here?' and that caused some laughter.

Dot sat behind the other children in the tea-tent. He drank half a glass of tea, sweetened for his childish palate; even so, the bitterness puckered and numbed his throat, and he was still forcing down sips when the others were burping and clattering their glasses back onto the tray.

The Bard took up the Three's box. He swung open the little brass door-hook, and the House sagged its pleated cardboard walls over his knee. Dot didn't know whether it was the House or the Bard that gave out the dry gasp.

The Bard closed his eyes. His hands and wrists grew very large and beautiful against his lamplit white robes. Dot had never seen the Bard work before, but now he saw, with a sip of the tea trickling and burning into his stomach, the state of excellence to which his mother's hands always aspired. The Bard had poor tools to work with – a broken box, puffing dust, two cow-bone keys – but his hands knew them so well that he could reach into the House and draw out, from its seemingly empty rooms, first Anneh, who was Mother of all mothers, then Robbreh, who began and ended Anneh's thrumming, and gave it shape and purpose

The Two were much, much louder right here in the tea-tent. Robbreh was in the ground, beating under Dot's seat, and in the air, thudding at his skull; Anneh was like black treacle dividing against his brow, streaming around his head.

By the time the Bard found Viljastramaratan in the deepest corner of the House, Dot was unable to think his own thoughts. Viljastramaratan, being coaxed out by the Bard's fine, giant hands, was like a string threaded with little blades, being pulled through Dot's head. The child spun and squealed and wheedled, pitching its voice higher and higher.

Around Dot, the middle-boys and the men closed their eyes and swayed on their seats. Their faces shone with sweat. As wide-eyed Dot saw this, he felt fear spring and steam and sprout all over him, so strong he could no longer lift the half-full tea-glass to his lips, for fear the child Viljastramaratan would notice him, would turn in its dance and show him its awful squealing face.

Very slowly the child's voice began to be muted, to giggle less, to be woven into the deeper and calmer songs of the Mother and the Father. There came moments when Viljas-tramaratan's voice was indistinguishable within the music, and those moments lengthened, until Dot realised with shivering relief that the child was gone for the night, leaving behind it space for Dot to be Dot again. He lifted the glass to his mouth, caught the whiff of nightmare on its lip, and lowered it again without sipping.

The music finished; the Bard closed up the House. He spoke, but relief was running so strong in Dot's veins that he hardly heard him; all he could think was how pleasant, how gentle and sensible the Bard's voice sounded, after Viljastra-maratan's racket, after the Mother's and Father's humming and beating. The Bard talked in a soft chant about the Three, and how all the goodness of the world fitted into this dusty box, the working mothers, the fathers steady at the centre with all the wisdom. And how all the evil of the world danced also out of this same box, like a swarm of children and madmen running wild through the streets of a big town.

To Dot, the Bard seemed to say the same thing over and over; he listened for the Three's names in the chant, hoping each time that this would be the last invocation. But the Bard showed no signs of ceasing, and the others still swayed and were silent, as if the Bard's voice were also a kind of awful music that was to be endured, and after a while Dot gave up hope and dozed off.

Very late in the night, he woke. The middle-boys were getting up all around him. Winsome's cousin Lute stooped for the tea-tray. Hurriedly, Dot clinked his glass onto the tray as it rose, when he had meant to replace it quietly when no one was looking. Yellow tea still swung in the bottom of the glass.

Lute looked from the glass to Dot. 'You have to drink all of it to see any Meaning,' he said scornfully, and he turned away with the tray.

Dot went home by himself and lay awake angry. All night, while he'd endured the singing, the women would have rocked babies by their own fire and murmured together, then one by one retired to sleep, when they chose. The house's starry eye looked down at him; his family's breathing – Ardent's thick and snuffly, Bonneh's steady – made the house seem alive, and he never wanted to leave the inside of that creature.

But that was middlehood, wasn't it? He wasn't a baby any more, was he? Wasn't a child. Dot curled up on his side and crooked his arm around his head, like Ardent, and fell asleep that way.

Dot didn't plan to leave. How could he? There never was such an idea. It was only that two days later, when the men came home from market, their returning woke Dot, and when they had settled, and there was no more movement outside, Dot was still awake. He rose and stood outside, under the tilted stars. And then he was walking without having decided to, following the fathers' trail, which was quite clear in the starlight. He carried nothing, not even a thought, away with him.

He reached the world midmorning. His body was stumbling with thirst and confusion by the time he saw the town's blocks and domes lifting out of the plain, but his gait firmed and his stance straightened as he approached them.

The market was over, of course, so the town was not the bustle he had expected. There were people about, but not a pushing crowd; there were animal-smells and food-smells, but they came one at a time as he passed along the streets, were not piled upon each other and inseparable. There were wonders – houses sheathed in pink-veined stone; penned animals feeding on bought-fodder; a purring, rolling vehicle that required no beast and no slope to move it. Every person wore the kind of cloth the Bard always railed against: a whirl of bright stripes with some emblem set all over – a crowned head, a burst of flowers, an embellished cake on a stand. And everyone wore gold or jewels about their person, the women great collars and earrings, the men heavy bangles and finger-rings. The more Dot saw of these adornments, the more he felt as if the Bard himself were walking at his shoulder, as if the old man was parading him, white-clothed and righteous through the evil world. Dot wanted to shake the Bard's hand off his shoulder; he wanted to hide in stripes and emblems himself. He wanted to be a gaudy townsperson, who if he saw the Bard shining along the street would find him strange, and cast him just such a curious look as that woman had given him through her fringe of beads, and bite back an uncertain greeting, as had that tall boy in the turmeric-yellow trousers and azure swing-shirt.

Dot had never felt so hungry. There was a drinking place in the empty square; he filled his belly with water and sat to collect himself. Then he walked on and on, almost to the far edge of the town, which took him until early afternoon. There he found a tree dangling mangoes at him over a wall, fruit lying ripe and burst open on the road below. Three mangoes, and his mind was a little less lost; he cleaned his face and hands at a pump and went on.

Shortly thereafter he came to a goat-pen. There were more goats in the pen than Dot had ever seen in his life. Leaning over the fence to admire them, he noticed, straight away, six or seven that were languid and scruffy about the mouth.

He went up to the man at the door of the house next to the pen.

'Who owns these goats, that they're let to be in such condition?'

'Why, the Baroness owns them,' said the man mildly. 'But what condition would that be?'

'Well, several are quite bad with the mouth-rot. You'll

want to get them some rash-leaf, if the herd is to see out the winter.'

The man was to become a friend called Kooric, but *My, what a blunt and old-fashioned way of talking you had back then,* he would say. But blunt or no, Dot knew more about goats than anyone in the Baroness's employ, and Kooric organised for him to be taken into her house. He was to learn worldly ways in return for his knowledge – knowledge of goats and gardens at first.

And of course, once your questions started, laughed Kooric, *no one could keep up with you! You must know everything that a merchant does, or a cleaner of wash-houses, or a soldier, or a weaver, or the children of the slums playing Devil-Dare; you must drive every jintny or tractor and visit every fair; you must be six hundred people in one!*

Show some kindness: he was starving, father, said Kooric's son Samed. *They had kept him pure and holy all his life, and now he must stuff his mouth with handfuls of dirt.* And he poked Dot mid-robe with a be-ringed finger.

It was on a visit to an even larger world that Dot found the House of the Many. Walking through the terrible rotten-water smell, the smoking-fish smell of Port-of-Lords, with Kooric and Samed, he saw it in a display window, on a stand covered with black velvet. Where the House of the Three was made of worn brown wood, the Many's seemed to have grown into its curves of blood-red glass, trimmed with silver lines. Where the Three's had two yellow teeth, the Many's bore a full set, dazzling plasticky white, slippery black and, at the other end, a grid of black buttons. Where the Three's rooms were joined with a cracked fan of brown paper that shed dust, the Many's had moist-looking red leather.

Dot went on careful feet to the window. The House glowed within. The Bard would abhor it; his beautiful hands would scorn to caress its newness. Where would be the virtue in making such easy music, with such a wealth of notes at your disposal? Dot had the feeling he was breathing in, and breathing in, feeding the laughter in his chest without ever letting it out.

Before too long, Kooric and Samed came back for Dot and moved him on, but that afternoon, while everyone slept, he came back to the shop to see if the House of the Many gave him the same feeling. If anything, it was stronger without the others there; he stood a long time with his hand on the glass, gently, inaudibly whooping to himself, gazing on the object that locked together the plainness of his past life, and the lustre and luxury of his present.

'You play accordion, do you?'

The man had come out of the shop, was halfway through a cigarette. He was as neat as the Bard, as sober-looking as the Bard, but dressed Western, in a dark suit and a white shirt, the tie the only jewel on him, a knot and band of ruby that changed to emerald with the light.

Dot shook his head and went on looking.

The man finished smoking. 'Come inside,' he commanded. 'I'll show you.'

Which is how Dot came to be seated under a window, drawing the Many out of their gorgeous House, easy as honey, multitudinous as the wavelets on the harbour-water. And how when night fell and the man released him, he walked back through the streets of Port-of-Lords with his ears full of the new music, and his eyes full of the little dusty place, the river-muddy place, where dwelt Winsome and those others, and Ardent, and Bonneh his mother.

He spent none of the money he had brought to Port-of-Lords, even while Samed and Kooric went mad in the markets, holding up cloths against him and urging him to buy. He held onto almost all his earnings in the next months until his second visit to the port, when he gave his savings to the accordion-man.

'Harsh country,' said Samed. His sunglasses had orange mirror-lenses that reflected the car windows, across which glided spine-tree and horizon.

'I suppose,' said Dot. 'Though I hadn't thought so until you said.'

'But there's nothing, nothing. It makes you thirsty just looking. And so boring.'

'Boring?' Dot laughed. 'You don't know boring. Boring to you is pausing between sweetmeats, or running out of women to woo.'

Samed grinned in a satisfied way under his blind orange eyes. He was dressed very gorgeously to go among the Bard's people. He hadn't believed there was a place, that wasn't a hospital, where people wore plain white. No one else had believed Dot, either, when he went hunting for white cloth to make his new, man's body – and Samed's as well – some Bard-clothes. The best he could do was plain Western white trousers and a loose-shirt with white-on-white embroidery. His arms felt light and naked without their rings and cuffs.

'Is that the place, sah?' said the driver.

'Already? Why, yes, it is. But go slowly!' Dot said alarmed. 'We're rushing towards it.'

And so they crept towards the houses, slowly enough for Dot to see piece by piece that things were not as they had been. The goat-pen had fallen in; there were only three goats tethered to posts among the houses. The Bard's house, the little one to which it had been such an honour and a terror to be summoned, was a broken half-cylinder of mud-bricks, all the thatch gone, nothing inside. The tea-tent on its slight rise was only the posts and strings and a few shreds of cloth blowing from the nails. Dot had forgotten how every thing, living or not, was the same milky-coffee colour.

'Oh, Dot,' said Samed. 'This is not a place for children.' Dot knew Samed was thinking of the garden he grew up in, a moist world of caves and ferns and pools and cushions, lit with the colours of everyone's clothes, set here and there with decorative town foods. He knew Samed was craving a guava-and-ice, in a tall glass with straws and a spoon. He knew that there was a good reason he had asked Samed to come, but caught here between his excitement and this sick feeling, he couldn't recall it; he thought he ought to have come alone, perhaps on foot, carrying nothing. He ought to have tried harder to find white cloth; even he was too odd and ornamented for this place.

They stepped out into a stunning white heat. Dot felt the pupils of his eyes contract, and was almost blind for a few moments. The driver switched off the engine, and Dot was deaf as well, his ears stuffed with the silence.

The shapes resolved into people beside their doors –

mothers and children only. From the farthest house emerged a mother with a rifle. She stood and assessed the car and the people who blossomed from it, then reached back into the house and propped the rifle there.

A mother came forward. A little one toddled after her, but was scooped back by its sister.

'Is that Dot I see?' asked the mother.

'Why, it's Winsome!' said Dot. 'Samed, remember I told you about— Winsome, meet my friend Samed.'

'I'm sure it's an honour,' said Samed smoothly. Winsome looked at him as if he had two heads.

'What has happened here, Winsome?' said Dot. 'Has the Bard died?'

She looked from Samed to Dot, even more disconcerted. 'No, not yet. At least, he hadn't when I left his food this morning.'

Dot looked around at the others, who had drawn forward in a crescent-shaped crowd to listen. He was very afraid of what else might have happened.

'And my mother?'

'She's in your house, where she always is.'

The little crowd broke open in that direction. A mother started to speak, but was hushed. None of them would meet his eye. Dot looked uncertainly at Winsome.

'Go on and see,' she said. Her little one had fixed itself to her leg, and she put her hand to its head.

Reassured, he went towards the house. His steps slowed at the smell. *They're all mad*, he thought. *This is some appalling joke, some punishment.*

'Mother?' he said into the smell at the door.

There was no answer. He folded himself into the house, the collapsing movements coming to him awkwardly in his man's body. Raw earth, dead fire, unclean flesh – all these underlay the worse smell. Dot moved away from the door to let the light show what it would.

His mother sat cross-legged and naked. Her hair was clipped back to silver speckles. She watched him as if he were a bantam that had run in by accident, as if her eyes just automatically followed anything that moved.

Then the thing at her feet came clear to him: not the loom he had thought, but Ardent's crooked legs. They didn't jerk or tremble in recognition of him, for there was no breath in her body. That worse smell came from her. The nails of the upstuck, misshapen hand were varnished silver; there was a bangle on the arm. Ardent's face was turned into the floor.

Dot's mouth found some home-tongue syllables. 'She was never meant to live out a full life, this one.'

His mother looked at him as if he had said something utterly without meaning. She spoke out of a throat that had not had food or water pass through it for a day or two. 'My daughter hasn't ever been sick in her life.'

Dot blinked away the woeful thought *Mother, do you not know me?* He nearly laughed. *Look at her*, he wanted to say, *she was born sick! She's sickness itself, just in the shape of a person. She was never meant to more than lie awhile here, then move on.* But you couldn't say that to the mother, could you? Not to the one who had tended Ardent, from the moment she was born a rubbery knot that couldn't be untied, to the moment she ceased to be however little of a self. Not to the person who had actually done that thankless, pointless work, with no more acknowledgment than a snuffle, with no more reward than another job of filth to clean up. Especially when you had walked away, yourself, from that work, walked away, without a thought, from that and all the other work of being among the Bard's followers. Walked away and not properly thought about that mother, or that work, for full years. And when you did think, waited further years before returning.

He went back out. Samed was seated in a crowd by the car. Children were taking off his rings and bangles and trying on his sunglasses. Mothers were laughing.

'How goes it, Dot?' he said.

'My sister is dead and needs burying.'

'This is the bent one?' said Samed.

Dot nodded. 'Winsome, is there a pick I may use?'

'Can I give these little ones their treats?' said Samed as Winsome led the way. 'Or at least play them some music? 'Cause I'll bet they're good dancers.'

'You go on and do that,' said Dot, relieved. He knew in this state, with this skirmish going on in his chest, he couldn't toss sweets to children, he couldn't bring out the Many and make them dance as he'd planned.

The gardens had shrunk to fit only the needs of these mothers and children. The walled grave compound had once been their centre; now it was their edge and you walked across bone-dry ground to reach it.

And the earth inside the walls was like concrete. After a few strokes, Dot took off his white-on-white shirt and relaxed into the work. It took a long time; Winsome brought him water and some sweetened cheese to fuel him. The little gusts of Samed's rich music, and children's cheers, and mothers' laughter – these too were like water and fresh blood to Dot's muscles.

Winsome came and sat with him. She talked into the grave rather than to him, brushing flies away all the while. 'Well, first the men left. That was maybe – oh, two years? – after you went away. The Bard tried to keep on. He took on everyone's wives – I myself have two children of him. But things got quarrelsome, and the Bard, he gave us up, all of us. He lives along the road in the old cowhouse now. We take him his food and drink, but he won't talk to us, and he won't have us talk to him. He says our high voices give him a pain in the head.' She smiled to herself, then saw Dot's dismay. 'No,' she said. 'He's not who he was.'

'I thought it would stay forever the same,' said Dot faintly, leaning on the pick.

'You shouldn't have gone,' said Winsome. 'We've talked about it. All the puff went out of him. You were the only one he could have handed on to, who wasn't blood-related, who wouldn't have caused quarrels.'

'What about Pedder?' But Winsome snorted. 'Or Lean Jo – they were the ones in line.'

'A line that never held firm.'

When the job was finished, Dot went to the river and washed. He put his shirt on and walked back up to the houses. Samed's party died down as he approached. Samed at the centre was the plainest Dot had ever seen him. Every child had some lump of jewel or gold upon it, but Samed's only adornment was the House of the Many, its crimson clashing joyfully with his yellow and orange robe.

'It's done,' Dot said lightly.

'All right,' said Samed, getting up. 'Now, children, it's time to be quiet and sad, isn't it, when a person has to put his sister in the ground. I'll play you some sad music, and we'll all go together, slowly, to the cemetery.'

Dot returned to his house. 'Better put on some clothes, mother. I've made a grave for Ardent, and we should take her there.'

Ardent was a lot smaller than he remembered, and lighter than he'd imagined she would be. Dot and Bonneh put her into her carry-bag, but then instead of putting her on Bonneh's back Dot carried her out of the house in his arms. Bonneh walked beside him, bare-armed in a night-shift, her hand on Ardent's head, and they proceeded slowly to the grave under the spell of Samed's music, slow and spare and sad.

Bonneh got down into the grave, and Dot knelt and passed Ardent down to her. She laid her in there, and drew the bag-string tight closed, and knotted it. Then Dot and Winsome helped her out and there was a silence, except for the low drone of Samed's music.

'You want to say something, Dot?' he said.

Bonneh was between Dot and Winsome, and they each held one of her hands in both of theirs. Dot looked over Bonneh's head to Winsome. 'I think you should speak, Winsome.'

'Oh, all right. Let me think. Ardent.' Samed gave her a little more music to think by, then faded it when she looked at him.

She began slowly, and left a pause between every phrase. 'Ardent, she had a short life, and some of us might think it wasn't much of one. But she felt the sun on her skin just like all of us do, and she tasted her food just fine; she smelt the smell of a good roasting fire, and of fresh rain just like us, and in her ears was the same birdsong. Best of all she liked the sound of people's voices and to have someone near. Her father died when she was very young, but he didn't run away and leave her the way a lot of kids' fathers have done. She had a mother, Bonneh, who was with her every day of her life. And also she had this brother, Dot; he spent his childhood with her. Sure, he left when he got to his middlehood – but then, didn't he come back? And isn't he here now, at her graveside?' Bonneh's grip tightened in Dot's hands.

'We'll start with the oldest, which is Safira. We'll each of us put a handful of earth in on Ardent. Then the kids will strip off and push the rest of the earth in, and then we'll all go down to the river and swim. And then, Dot's friend Samed says he's got some treats, so we'll have something of a feast, and drink to Ardent's life, and welcome Bonneh back from her place of mourning.'

Samed swelled the music, and Safira came forward. 'I knew you would say the right things,' said Dot.

'Better than the Bard ever did,' said Bonneh between them, watching the earth fall to the carry-bag. 'He would have preached all over her and spoiled it.'

Towards the end of the feast, Dot walked away to the cow-house. The sun was lower and the world not so painfully bright.

'Bard Jo?' he said into the slatted darkness of the wooden hut. 'It's Dot here.' And he went in.

The boards chopped up the darkness with planes of dusty sunlight. After a few moments the old man became visible on his bed against the far wall. His pale foot-soles pointed to the ceiling, and the pattern of his blanket was interrupted by his thin dark frame. He was lying on his back, breathing out illness from some serious place inside him; the hut was thick with the smell, which was of dead Ardent, with rotting wet lung added.

'I came back for a visit, Bard,' said Dot. If he called him by name, perhaps he could believe this really *was* the Bard.

The breathing worked up to speech, through spittle and twigs in the Bard's throat, it sounded like. 'It was Dot, was it, playing that great *layer-cake* of a music?' Sweet cakes being things of evil and not proper food.

'No, Bard,' said Dot, into the horrible withering wind of the Bard's disgust. 'It was my friend Samed. But we both play.'

You must not retire like that, Kooric had told him after his first fight with Samed. *You mustn't bow your head and take it. You must speak back. You must not take Samed's rubbish.* But here in the Bard's presence – even the failed Bard, even the corruptible Bard – keeping his back straight, and the idea of speaking, felt mannered and arrogant.

'And you'll have brought some rubbish for the children?'

'A few bits of shine, Bard. Nothing harmful—' He heard the fatal weakness of apology in his voice.

'What would *you* know?' The Bard jolted on the bed. 'So harmed yourself, so prettied up, so taken in by all the shine and the music and the *fun*. Did you think it would be *fun*, to bring your worldly friends here, to amaze them with how spare and poor you used to be? To walk in like a god and scatter gifts, like a *father*, you thought?'

The Bard spat into something that had already been spat in many times.

He's too clever a man, thought Dot, in the grip of the old fears. *He's too clever and too right. He knew me when I was only myself without any world-trappings.*

'The only father I knew never scattered gifts. He came home angry. He washed the town off himself as quick as he could—'

'That's not your father,' said the Bard in a scribbly hiss. 'Don't try and claim that one.' He cleared his clogged voice and spat again, and Dot could see and hear him shaking his head against the pillow.

'Like I say, he was the only one—'

'*Your father*—' The Bard hoisted himself upon one rail of an arm, that was ragged with either flesh or shirt, Dot couldn't tell which. A slat of light bounced off his yellow-white hair, and made a faint glow on the wall. 'You knew your father just fine; he led you away from here as if he had a halter on your neck. He sent you back to us, all hung about and decorated with his cloths and jewels – you may think it's you, but it's just Morri Simpsim, making trouble again. All that's missing is the bullet-belt and the foreign gun. And the soldier mates hanging off him for his money's sake. The feeble mind is the same. Why could you not have grown up strong, like your mother, worthy of Bonneh as no other man could be – not even *I*.' He fell back on the bed, breathing hard. The golden dust above him swirled.

There was other furniture in the cow-house. There was a

wooden chest on Dot's right. An unlit lamp stood on it, and beside it the Three's House, hooked closed.

'I am sure my mother has always respected and admired you,' he said.

'And I am sure she has not, for how could she? I was an embarrassment with my wives and my slave-men and my "wisdom". I preached purity and lived a prince's life. Bonneh preached nothing and lived purity. Her vow held her steady, and not all my glamour and power could ever budge that woman. She was before me as my lesson every day, yet did I ever learn?'

The Three's House was quite a lot smaller than the House of the Many – but then, everything here had shrunk with the years: the curve of the river, the mothers, the Bard himself. Dot took the House to the doorway where he could see it. Oh, yes – smaller, and so much lighter. So brown, so worn. Even the healing hands of the accordion-man in Port-of-Lords could do nothing for this. It hardly *existed* as an instrument.

'Take it,' rasped the Bard. 'Take the damned thing. Everything else you've taken, you might as well.'

'Can it still sound?'

'As much as it ever did. Go on, take its weight off my mind. And your weight, too. Leave me to die in peace and with nothing.'

Dot left the cow-house and walked back up the road to the village. Samed had got the balloons out; bright dots of colour were bounding and flying at the end of strings. There was a tiny pop as one burst, then a tiny child-wail. Dot held the dusty accordion to his chest, where he knew its ancient concertina-folds would leave long stripes of disintegrating paper. He felt haggard from exposure to the Bard's bitter breath; his belly was sore from the tension it had carried all day.

He walked up the rise to the remains of the tea-tent. The tables and benches were weather-warped but still strong, and he sat where the last piece of worn cloth would shield him from the village. The breeze was very soft and steady, the sunlight yellow-gold, the shadows long.

He undid the catch. It was a while since the accordion had been used; Dot had to open it very carefully so that it didn't tear itself apart, so that the fragile cardboard didn't split in several places and take away the instrument's last breath. He eased it open and closed slowly several times, wondering whether it could play a single note without breaking.

And as he wondered and worked the house's hallway, Anneh idled out a side-door of the house just as she always had, her arms full of thatch, three piglets and a chicken following behind. She could go only so far, to the limits of her yard and beyond that to her farm patch, a bit farther, a bit fainter, before she faded from hearing.

Robbreh took some finding, some odd angles and pressures, but before too long Dot had him singing, and not long after that the two of them singing together, going about their separate businesses. Dot had tried for the same sound on the red accordion, but there was too much juice in it, too much harmony, not enough dust and age. The broken pieces that made the Three alive were missing.

Then, in the middle of one of Robbreh's wheezes he heard a corner, an edge of an echo that was high and crazy and said anything that came into its head. He played more of the same part of Robbreh, coaxing and coaxing the little one out from behind the dad.

What was left of the flap of the tea-tent lifted, and there stood Bonneh, washed and dressed in her white. She came in and perched on a bench, inclined her head and listened. From his years out in the world, Dot read her movements as full of grace, the bones of her face and speckled head as smooth and beautiful.

'Been a long time since anyone took that up,' she said in a pause where Dot had lost the older Two and was working to find them again among the huffs and rattles. They jumped out again suddenly with Viljastramaratan blaring beside them, and Dot had to laugh, and his mother too smiled.

He played until he had all three moving somewhat in the old ways, Anneh busy with her work, Robbreh happy among the rumble of the men.

But Viljastramaratan came and went as Viljastramaratan pleased. When that one decided to sing, Dot could keep him going a little, but—

'I can't keep a hold on the child,' he said to Bonneh.

She gave the smallest smile in the world, rose and left the tent. And when the fraying flap had fallen closed behind her, he wound the music down and finished. The wind in the cloth and the guy-ropes had more notes in it than the accordion, though it didn't form what you'd call music.

Dot fastened the Three's House closed and carried it down to the village. The shadows streamed away, endlessly long now. A sweet-wrapper tinkled past him. The car stood beyond the huts, its curves gathering the last sunlight into lines and points. Samed was walking slowly towards it like a carnival in his orange robe, the children running up to replace his rings and bracelets. He flirted with the mothers over the children's heads, and they bumped shoulders with each other and laughed behind their hands.

But in the car, against the sunset, Dot saw Bonneh's round head. Like the plainest wooden statue, she sat polished by life's handling, beautified by the completion of her work. She waited while he wrapped and stowed the old accordion, while he said farewell to Winsome, and warned her children not to put these gifts of rose-scented soap in their mouths. She waited motionless while he went to the fields' edge and stood over the fresh mound where Ardent lay, which the children had prettied with lolly-foils weighted with stones. When Samed and Dot entered the car, she eyed them out of a deep smiling thought, and then fixed her gaze forward again.

'Bonneh, aren't you bringing belongings?' said Samed. 'Your . . . your pots and things? Other clothes, maybe?'

Again she cast him that sideways joking glance and was silent.

'Samed,' said Dot. 'You are my best friend, but you don't know when to keep quiet.'

'Is there such a time?' laughed Samed. He took his sunglasses from a child's hand poked through the window, and tried to kiss the hand before it was snatched away.

Dot tapped the driver on the shoulder. 'We can go now,' he said.

wooden bride

I'm in danger. Up ahead, limousines, white horses, flower strewers, white-and-silver gift carts block the street. Here, brides and their families crowd. Irate mothers are shouting, fathers are giggling and some are trying to push forward; we brides stand motionless in First Position, like fence posts in a flood. But a few feet behind me, Gabby's dad has started one of his hairy stories. In many a Composure class I've busted out laughing from one of those stories. But this is The Day; I can't afford to come unstuck today. I have to get away from him, before the crowd jams up completely.

I turn, and people make way for me. 'Why,' says Gabby's dad in his always-surprised voice, 'if it isn't little Matty Weir!' I steel myself for the joke he'll toss at me, that'll prod my mind in an unexpected spot and make me splutter laughter. But it doesn't come, and I pass through. I lost Gabby's dad for words! I won't risk blushing by thinking about such a compliment now; I'll store it away to tell Mother and Winke later, when I'm allowed to be myself.

Here, I'll duck into the Lanes district. I haven't been through this part of town since they rebuilt after last year's rat-hunt, but it can't be that different, can it? And there won't be a lot of people around; not many families in these poorer quarters can afford to bride-up a daughter.

I gather up two handfuls of the beaded, white-tissue skirt. Last night's rain has left all the flagstones gleaming, and the sun shows up every pore of them, every puddle and scrap of refuse. I tiptoe through.

The slippers are made to last one day – *this* day. They're folded out of varnished paper, with a twinkle in it. We had to go all the way to the markets at the Crossways to find a paperbinder who did shoes the old way with no glue, just sheer skill of folding and knowledge of a girl's own foot and a girl's own walk holding the creation together.

Where am I, now?

The crowd noise is fading behind me, though the bells still carol overhead. Oh yes, there's the old Mechanics Hall, where Mother used to hold her mask-making workshops, so I turn right here to loop around the Orphans Home. I'm trying to hurry, yet stay Composed. I'm keeping my skin cool, all pores closed, as they taught us in School. I'll come up to the side door of the church, by the Hospice there. It won't matter to Mother and Winke; they can still come up the main way and do their nodding and smiling. That's not the point of this, for me. I'm not quite sure what the point *is* – I couldn't put it into words or anything – but it's strong, and it's not about getting the neighbours to admire me. The neighbours have nothing to do with it at all.

What, have they *moved* the Orphans Home? Come to think of it, I did hear Gabby and Flo say something about that. Farther up the hill, for better drainage. But the lane looks much the same – maybe a bit of a curve downward, which I'll have to compensate for when I get to Farmers Bar. Those bells, they're wild, as if they're shouting fire, or an attack on the town; they're a test in themselves. But I'm prepared for that kind of test: I've got counting rhymes in my head; I've got breathing exercises; I've got six terms worth of Bride School resources to draw on.

And then the bells stop, and the lane stops. And I stop. Farmers Bar isn't here.

'That doesn't make sense,' I say coolly, firmly. 'No matter how ratty, a public house doesn't move. They smoke out the cellars, and they scrub everything else down with disinfectant.'

Then I remember: it was the Olds Home that moved, not the Orphans; they moved all the olds away from the dampness, for their arthritis or something. The Orphans Home should have been where it always was.

Five lanes meet where I'm standing; not a soul stirs along any of them. Not a sound from any window or door.

'It's all right,' I say, counting furiously inside to keep my heart down. 'I can go back the way I came.'

But behind me are two lanes, and with all my revolving I can't remember which one I came down.

'The church is at the top of the hill, Mattild.' There's a shake in my voice, and I pause to do some breathing. 'All you have to do is choose any lane that goes upward, and you'll be there.'

So I set off. Actually, the silence – just the pat and shush of my shoes – is more alarming than the bells were. The silence means they're inside the church – all the brides, anyway. The relatives will take a while to shuffle in. But I mustn't think about that; I must just walk and breathe and count.

Every lane deceives me; every lane curves. I set out confidently upward at every corner; I end up hoisting my skirts behind me so they won't drag as I go down steps. Lanes keep ending at a wall, or a dripping mill-wheel, or they continue on the other side of an unbridged drain a trousered person could leap, but not me in my finery. I go back and forth, breathing, counting, intent on outwitting the Lanes. I try a new tactic, taking some downward streets in the hope that their curves will take me upward. No such luck; down and down they go. I'm so confused, I'm just starting to think I'm getting somewhere when I arrive – the lane does a quick turnabout and dumps me – at an arched gateway in the town wall.

I stand there, counting, breathing, shocked. Beyond the gate, the water meadows and the market gardens stretch purple and many-greened among their windguards of black pines. Rubbish-stink streams from the pits farther east.

Ha! said my dad over the whirr and clatter of his workshop. I was there to wangle money out of him towards my shoes. *My daughter? Matty Weir? Miss Million-Miles-an-Hour? Miss Ten-Projects-at-Once, none of them ever finished? You haven't a hope! You're lucky to've made it through the first semester. They mustn't have much of a crop this year.* All this very cheerfully, as he *zizzed* the wooden bowl to a perfect curve on the lathe.

And then Mother, wearing that face that makes you ashamed to have brought her down from the clouds where she dances and sings and brings such joy to so many people – that doubtful, older face: *But are you sure about this?*

Which I was, I *was*. Tearfulness rises in my throat. My skin trembles, ready to give out. I was *sure* I was sure, until . . .

An old woman in blue gardening clothes appears in the archway, carrying an enormous cabbage. 'Madam,' she says, and walks in past me.

Madam, she said, not *Miss*. You see a bride, you don't meet her eye. You say *Madam* to acknowledge her, but nothing more unless she speaks to you. Thank the Saints that woman came along.

I breathe more carefully. My shoes are still good – perhaps a bit soft underfoot, but still good. I just need to walk out a little way beyond the arch to see which gate I'm at, to see my way back.

I lift my skirts and go. I'm not far out among the fields before I can see the church's twin spires. But I'm behind them; if I take any of the three gates I can see from here, I'll be straight back in the maze. Better to go around on the outside to a gate that leads to straighter streets, like Silk Street or Jewellers Way. I shade my eyes and pick out a zigzag way for myself, along the broad earthen field-walls, between the water meadows and the moving leaves of purple sour-kale.

I put out of my head the thought of Mother and Winke and all the other families in the church, sitting patched pink with rose-window light. I push away the vision of all the other brides, their upper bodies like snooty white flock-herons at rest on a mist of white gorgeousness. I just walk, swiftly and calmly, trying to think of nothing.

You see, said Mother doubtfully, *as someone who had to go to Bride School herself, whose parents wanted it more than anything else in the* world, *I sometimes thought* . . .

113

It was as if her voice were *funnelling* stubbornness and resentment into my spine.

You see, the kings and queens that it's modelled on, they're just so long dead; they have so little to do with our lives now. They're four revolutions ago – think about that! And what were those revolutions about?

I spoke through gritted teeth. *I don't* care *what they were about—*

About people being able to relax, and move any way they wanted, and find their own path creatively. They were about freedom.

She was in full flight and making perfect sense. I had to stop her before she deflected me. *Which doesn't mean,* I said gaspingly – I had no control over my breathing, back then – *which doesn't mean the Straitened kings and queens were all bad. I mean, people must have let them rule because they believed the way they lived* worked *in some way, don't you, think? It's not as if they revolted after six months – those royals had power for hundreds of years! If everybody hates you, you can't last that long.* I think I made a pretty good fist of it, considering I hadn't even been to the Bride School Open Day yet.

Mother was too smart for me. Dad just laughed at me. Once I got through the entrance tests, all I had on my side was stubbornness. I couldn't explain it to myself any more than I could to them. I listened; I agreed; but I dug in my heels. *It's just something I'm* Going To Do, I said. *I've never imagined not doing it. I've always meant to.* That was all I had.

Bit by bit, the zigs and zags of the field-walls work me farther from the town. The spires turn, and the façade comes into view, the rose-window with the Saints' linked crowns above it. But it seems to be moving farther away, not closer. The fields' silence takes over, plopped more silent by fish, creaked more silent by breeze-shifted cabbage-leaves, startled quieter by a burst of bird out of reeds. Always there are people at middle distance or beyond, bending to the water, to the feet of the plants, wading in mirages.

This gentle, shoe-protecting walk is tiring after a while. I'm glad when I reach my friend Yakkert's village, with its wide, flat path, where I don't have to carry my skirts to protect my hems. My hands feel raw from that, after two years of oiling and gloving them, two years of keeping them safe from cuts and callouses.

People are laundering at the water-race on the common. At tables outside the house-doors, children and old people are picking over dried cornsilk to make their votive dollies. 'Madam,' says anyone I pass near, and they lower their eyes. They all know me, and I them. Two years ago I used to come out here to fish the race regularly; I've made so many dollies with these people, I could do it in my sleep. But none of them will greet me by name while I'm dressed like this.

My skin feels thin, ready to perspire. It's not that I *care* whether they talk to me. I can come back tomorrow and they'll be as friendly as ever. I sit on a stump and Yakkert's cat, Biddy, comes up to me. A cat's not to know you can't approach a bride, is she? I give her a bridely stroke of the head, instead of wrestling her over and pushing my face into her belly-fur, as I usually would.

Yakkert's mother passes in front of me and leaves a pottery cup of cool tea on the next stump. She knows I'm supposed to save my mouth for bishop's cake and wedding wine. But she wouldn't – no one here would – think less of me if I drank that tea.

Which isn't the point, I tell myself as the circle of sky on the tea-surface stills from its rocking. *Besides, it's enough that she's put it there. I don't have to actually drink it to get the benefit.*

I stand up and check my skirt-hems. At the back, the edges are grey-brown and damp from brushing the dew and the ground. And the outer edge of one shoe is sodden, in spite of my careful walking. I'll have to walk differently, oddly, so it doesn't get any worse. I could take the shoes off and go barefoot and faster. I could bundle up my skirts and run, and probably reach the church before the brides leave. Why can't I find it in myself to do that?

Because it would be me, Miss Matty Weir, who never finishes things, who never does things quite right, who'd be running. It would be the person everyone expects me to be, the person everyone thinks I am.

I gather up some skirt into my sore hands, and walk away from the village. You just keep up the Bridal Gait, Mattild. Though it be among weeds and the trickle of leaking water-gates, instead of across petals and floor-wax, you step and step until you get where you said – through six terms of homework and gown-fittings and gossip and abstinence-from-all-fun – where you said you were going to go. You might not get to smell the incense, or hear the pure drone of the Wedding Song from the choir, or see the visiting bishop in his magnificent tarnished ancient robe, his rings all over car-buncles. But you set yourself on this path to becoming some-one not Matty, someone cool and unflustered, remote, with impermeable skin. And you'll get there – with measured steps you'll get there.

'Madam,' say a string of gardeners' children. Each carries a puppy in one hand and a basket of sorted eggs in the other. The sun has lost all its morning kindness, lifting into steam, killing off the breeze. It stings through my sheer sleeves and on my neck, which is usually covered by my mess of hair. My skin feels cool, though; I'm keeping it that way.

The bells shout again. In the church the brides will be losing some of their Composure – they've only the photographs to go, and then they can all fall away down the porch stairs, blessed and brilliant and allowed to laugh now, to wreck their dresses, to show their legs, to hug their families. The feast awaits in flower-stuffed halls around town: many-storeyed white cakes, powder-blue wedding cachous, flavoured violets, glazed fruit, clove-studded meats, salt-crusted heart-biscuits.

Paths go off to right and left, among dank slabs of mirror whiskered with rice. But no path seems to lead to the mound of the town – not straightly, anyway. But I'll get there, even if *not* straightly. The bishop must stay for the feasting; if the worst comes to the worst he can bless me among flowers, between mouthfuls of cake, with cake-cream on his beard.

When finally I reach the gate I want and step out of the meadows, the town streets are empty, dim and very cool. The higher I climb, the more flower-petals are gummed to the flags, the more constant are the gusts of chatter and music channelled along the lanes. I know exactly where I am and how to avoid those halls, the sight of food, the cries of brides with unpinned hair. My leg aches from my toe gripping the loose shoe; my hands are stiff from carrying the netting skirt; my arms cramp from lifting all the expensive cloth.

The church is stripped of its usual pennants and garlands. The church square, too, is bare of all decoration. Of all the people who choked the streets this morning, only the photographer is left, folding his black cloth on the church steps.

I rustle across the square. All those Posture, Carriage, Masque and Step lessons play themselves out in me as if I have no will of my own. The boned bodice holds my back right, and my face is rightly wooden, empty of anything – weariness, anxiety, relief, determination, anything.

The photographer glances aside from his equipment case. He sees the stained edge of my skirt and pauses.

'Mr Pellisson,' I say in my cold, rehearsed Bride-Voice.

'Madam.' His gaze remains lowered.

'I require your sponsorship. Is the bishop within?'

'He is, Madam.' He closes his case with a soft, rich click. Wordlessly he precedes me up the steps.

The church is very dark, its air like cold water. It seems much larger than usual, cleared of all candles, all votives, banners, flowers. All the cosiness is gone, and the building's ribs rise naked to separate the high lattice windows. A vein of light runs up the central aisle, a carpet of white petals. Someone is sweeping them from the altar towards us; he slips into a side-aisle and murmurs 'Madam' as we pass.

We reach the altar. All the monstrances with their yellowed Relics have been taken away, all the cloths and vases and prayer-trees. The only ornament is the Saint-Crown on its purple cushion on the altar, two palace guards in ceremonial black like statues either side. The only scent is of cold marble.

The photographer opens the brass altar-gate for me. The cold strikes straight up through my damp paper shoes.

We skirt the altar and enter the vestry, which is smaller, warmer, carpeted, and full of the cedar smell of vain old man. The lace trim on the hem of the bishop's under-robe – well, none at my School could afford such stuff. I mustn't meet his eye, mustn't look for the outer vestments, the thorned mitre. I must keep my eyes on the red carpet, the expensive hem, the gilded paper slipper-toe.

A plain wooden kneeler is pushed in front of me. Pellisson's hand plucks a leaf from the beading near my hem and withdraws.

I kneel, and the bishop starts the blessing: *Witness: To the holy basilica of All Saints comes this young woman, beloved of the town of Mountfort-among-the-Waters* . . . He doesn't need the vestments, this man; the words vest him, vest all three of us as beautifully as the robes would. He shapes his voice to set the small, padded vestry singing.

. . . *before witnesses that she has undergone instruction and proven herself constituted of such purity of body, austerity of practice, modesty of habit and restraint and moderation of temperament as befits* . . .

How many times have I read those words in the liturgy-book? How many times have I stopped and said to myself, *That isn't me. I'm just not like that, moderate and pure and austere. I'll never make it through; they'll stop me* way *before the Day when a bishop would say those words over me. 'What were you thinking, Matty?' they'll say, and laugh, and send me to the cashier to claim back the rest of the School fee.* Yet here I am, relaxed in the flow of the holy words, firm in the rightness of this, taking the blessing and knowing – as I haven't known for two whole years, as I didn't even know this morning, darting out of the house because I hadn't the patience to wait for Mother to dress Winke's hair; as I didn't know pacing the Lanes and counting – that it's mine to take, that I deserve it, that I've earned it. I've made myself a Bride; out among the fields today, alone and without instruction, I wedded myself to the severe and lovely ways of the old dead kings and queens at their height, when all the people loved them. And now the bishop's thumb is dipping into the sacred oil and ash – ash that once, centuries ago, was actual kingly or queenly matter – and he's whispering to himself the final and most secret words, in the language of the Straitened times, and applying history to my brow.

Pellisson helps the bishop take the bride-book from its box. They place it on its stand, and the bishop unlocks and opens it. He moves aside the gilded bookmark, and there's Agnes Stork's flourish that she practised for two years, and Felicity Doe's loopy tangle of a name, with the two hearts dotting the i's. When the quill is readied and handed to me, *Mattild Weir,* I write plainly, so that anyone who looks will know that I was here, became a Bride, this day. Thereunder signs my witness: Pellisson, descended all the way from the court painters of the Straitened days.

The way to thank the bishop is with money, in a white purse a bride unties from her waist. He opens a chest and the bride-purses are piled in there like sleeping mice. A few are trimmed end to end with lace, one or two monogrammed;

most are like mine, standard-issue Bride School purses, plain linen, strongly sewn.

I give an exemplary curtsy, nothing ostentatious. Rising, I look at the bishop properly for the first time. His face is round and red and weary. His white comb-over has a mitre-furrow around it. Apart from the white, double-plaited beard, he's greatly ordinary against the magnificent vestments in their case behind him, the gold ribbons of the mitre laid just so on the shoulders of the cape.

The bishop tips his head at me, saying *get-out-of-here* as much as *nicely-executed-curtsy-bless-you-my-child*.

Now the Bride walks ahead of her sponsor, out into the body of the church, down the darkened aisle, past the glowing heap of petals at the rear.

Out on the church steps, Pellisson scatters handfuls of petals around my feet. My eyes fix on the middle distance as a good bride's should, but I can still see him: he backs down the steps without needing to check his footing. He shakes out his black cloth and organises his photographer's dust. My spine is straight as a pine trunk and my face is empty of everything.

He arranges all his equipment, and then he comes up the stairs and starts to arrange *me*. It only strikes me then how unsupervised I am, as his gentle adjustments of the hem tug at my waist. There's no crowd of matrons making sure the thing's done right, snapping commands at him, or sighing and coming forward to fix me themselves. But he knows what he's doing; he knows about cloth; he knows with small and professionally exact movements how to tease the maximum width, the maximum puff, out of the skirts, the maximum contrast with my slender-fied, rigidified upper half.

121

'Is all satisfactory?' I say – for he may not speak unless spoken to.

He steps back to judge. 'If Madam would lift her chin just a touch higher?'

She would. Although she could hug Pellisson, old vinegar-bottle that he is, Madam would be pleased instead to lift her chin, to look down her regal nose past His Nobody-ness.

He disappears under the cloth. The dust flashes and thuds. The smoke jumps free like a loosed kite.

earthly uses

'Get dressed, boy,' says Gran-Pa, shaking me awake. 'You're going for a long walk.' He stands over me with the lamp while I pull on my trousers and shirt – clothes he won't wear any more, they're so stained and frayed. Under his other arm is one of our cheeses, all wrapped in its fancy market-paper.

'Where am I off to?' I'm doing up my boots, the leather of which is nailed down to the soles.

'To find me one of them angels.'

I straighten up and stare.

'Get on with it!' he growls. I duck to my boot-tying 'You'll go up the foothills and in at the gorge, and you'll call one.'

'Hunh? How?' I say before thinking.

He stamps his foot nearly on me. 'How would I know, swivel-head! Have I ever summoned one?'

Over on her bed, my Gran-Nan moans, and Pa doesn't go on, only breathes a few times as if he would. Then his voice drops to a murmur. 'You'll call one. And you'll give it this cheese. And you'll bring it back here, for your nan.'

I finish my boots. His face is Like That.

'Back here to this house,' I say.

He holds out the cheese.

I take it and stand up. His eyes are a little lower than mine, when I'm in boots and he's not.

'Fast as you can,' he snaps. 'She won't last long.'

I look to Nan, the little lump of her in the bed. Her sickness rottens the air. I punch Pa in the shoulder to make him face me. He totters, open-mouthed. 'And you,' I say, 'you leave her *right alone* 'til I get back. Not a word. Not a touch. Or I'll axe you, you murderer.'

And I swing away. The full distance to the trees, I expect the axe between my shoulderblades myself.

He's an old man and cranky, but he's all I've got, so I must put up with him, mustn't I?

He's not *all*, actually. It's just that Nan, being so small and grey and quiet, seems like a cooking and housekeeping part of *him*, not really her own self. She used to be her own, when I was a little lad. She was never what you'd call lively, she was never strong or jolly, but she wasn't so utterly broken by Pa's treatment that she couldn't issue me some ration of kindness. It may have been quiet and hidden; it may have been the barest, meanest ration a child could get by on; still I remember it, and if Pa has all my fear and dread, Nan has what little love I bear towards either of them.

Anyway, what's surprising me now is: he's never had patience for angels. At their merest mention he'll get shouty.

'Don't talk to me about those things!' he'll bellow. 'What blamed use are they to anyone? What's worse, they take perfectly good working men and women, and flap their foul wings over them and make them hermits, or wise-women, or prating poets. "Ooh, the *eenjels* made me do it." "Ooh, the *eenjels* told me to drop all my worldly work and stop paying my taxes, and throw my fambly away like you shake a bit of dog-dung off your shoe" – and fly off over the fields like a butterfly, no doubt. And live in the wild, hey, on those bowls of stew,' he'll cackle, 'that nestle under bramble-bushes, and those warm loaves that dangle off the trees—'

'And they *smell*!' he always finishes, as if that's the final thing about them that no one can get past. 'They stink like bad potatoes and death.' And he spears a chunk of meat with his fork and plugs his ranting mouth with it. As if he isn't sitting there in his sweaty breeks and jersey, whoofy as a tomcat himself. As if his boots aren't thrown down at the door, caked in pig-reek.

And Nan nods all righteous: 'That's true, too. Foul beasts.'

I smelt angels once, when I was chasing that young sow up the foothills. The sow's flattened-grass trail had begun to wander; it was forgetting to flee, drawn off by all the wild food smells – that's always a pig's undoing. I'd be on it soon.

The angels caught me side-on, like fox-scent catches a hunting-dog and bends its poor brain. *Bad potatoes?* Hmmm. More like, having mouldy dung forced so far up your nose that it starts tearing out the back of your throat. *Death?* It was more like – I tell you, I'm cramming a pumpkin into an eggshell, putting that smell in words.

Just as that poor sow did, I went wandering away from my purpose, hunting whiffs of angel-stink through the undergrowth. I was all nose for a while. And it was hard going, without the pig breaking a path for me. Finally, all pulled about and decorated with dead leaves and spider webs, I came to where I could see them ahead, in a clearing. The grass there was well flattened, in some places worn away to shiny earth.

It was like watching two skin tents tangled up together, steaming and rocking. Bit by bit I made sense of them: stretched-leather wings; spine-bumps in two matching curves; glints of horns in their matted brown hair; hindquarters without sex or hole of any kind.

'They're always red,' says Pa, 'blushing and flushing. It's not seemly. And their eyes – you look in and there's no one in there that's like a normal man – they're just bright and bright, and empty.'

I didn't see eyes that day, and didn't want to. Even walking here through the angel-less darkness, the power of not-wanting-to-see-eyes makes me swerve and shake my head. The fighting was quite enough. The fighting and the foreign bodies, bodies of not-people, doing who knew what. It was like running from knot-hole to knot-hole in the back wall of Yoman's barn at the spring musical, spying on the couples in the hay. I'd shriek like I knew what I was seeing, but there'd be an awestruck, silent *why* inside me along with everyone else, the very middle, real, unpretending part that didn't understand. I'd never seen anything quite so far outside my ken as these fighting angels – mine, and Pa's, too, whose lead on worldly matters I'd dumbly followed ever since he and Nan took me in. Followed without thinking.

Those angels started me thinking; their smell was like crushed mint to my brain, breathing open huge new spaces there that I'd not the faintest notion how to fill. They rocked about, twigs and dirt sticking to their sweaty red backs and wings. I couldn't see how they'd ever end it, this fighting, this sexing, whatever it was, was so locked, the two were so near equal in weight and passion. And Pa's sow was waiting just around the corner. And Pa was at home totting up the loss to his market-day grog-money. If these beasts broke apart, if they noticed me, if anything changed or developed from this clearing, I'd be lost to the world of slops and chores and earthly breeding forever. I was too sensible a lad to wait, despite the new worlds gathering under my nose. I fought away from the clearing.

When I got back, Pa was too relieved about the sow to notice I was different, and busy ordering me this way and that to strengthen the pen. He's powerful with words, Pa; in a flash he can make his shoddy building job your fault, and he'll work you hard to punish you.

I never told Pa I saw them, and I never talked about angels in any way that would make him think I had.

It's not a difficult journey. I've hunted in these foothills all my life. I could reach the gorge in pitch-darkness, using the feel of the land underfoot, and this moon is as good as noon-tide sun to me, sliding over the treetops. When I come near the place where I saw the fighters, I can feel my brain beginning to bend again, as it always does when I come by here. Would they be fighting now, straining and rolling in the night? Are they fighting all the time, keeping the earth polished with their sweat?

But there's the gorge to think of, and there's this grand cheese to deliver. Furthermore, there's Nan, isn't there? I force my wayward head beyond that place.

*

Every spring when the forest was budded-up and beautiful, Nan used to take me to a clearing, like the angel-clearing, only under a cliff. She'd hold my hand tight as she walked me out of the brush onto the hardened rolled earth. She'd say nothing while we were there; she'd put out the lunch she'd brought for herself, on its opened paper; she'd draw me back into the scrub. One last look behind and we'd leave. When we were back to the path she'd take a deep relieved breath, and start to talk, about anything and everything but what we'd just done.

'But how many times have you seen them, Pa?' I asked him, next time the topic of angels came to our table.

'Enough to know they're no good. Enough to know that those women as sings to them and makes prayers and pilgrimages is talking through their skirts. There's nothing *holy* about those things; they're not *sacred*.' Sacredness itself was a bad taste in his mouth; he spat it out, and holiness, too.

'So you've seen them lots of times, then? When there was that plague of them, you said?'

'Not here, that wasn't,' he was quick to say. 'That plague was over past the mountains, in junglier land where the weather's good and sweaty for them. They'd never breed up big in these parts; it's too cold.'

'So how'd you see yours?' I was sure to sound admiring and curious.

'At a distance,' he finally admitted. 'Over the gorge, like eagles. Only, of course, a different shape, and so big.'

'So a whole flock of them, like gunney-birds?'

'Nah, just the one.' He made busy with his food.

'Oh, but that wasn't the only time?' I was all caution, you'd have thought.

'Well, there was that dead one. All pulled to pieces like any carcass, by scavengers. I tell you, it stank less than the live ones do.'

'So they have bones like us, and flesh that gunneys can feed on?'

'Of course they do. What did you think they was made of, sugar and starlight? You been listening to those women, uh? You been off in a corner with your nan, whispering?' He chewed as he jeered at me. Nan looked into her lap.

''Course not.' I hunched down over my plate, as if embarrassed, but really I was all aglow. Why, he'd only seen a corpse and one in the distance. I'd seen two, up close, and fighting! There weren't many times I could better Pa, but that was one of them. What's more, he didn't know to beat me for it.

Children like me often run away to the angels – children who have it worse than me, whose grandparents beat them every day, instead of just at low times, or starve them so badly they think they can manage better on fog-berries and starch-root. In the days after I saw the angels, I was in a real turmoil of understanding those children. I could see myself going back while the pig-trail was still there, while the scrub was still broken through to the fighting ground; in my mind I walked up there – then and later – whenever anything happened at the house, whenever any change or accident or turn of the wind put Pa in a bad frame of mind, even after the trail would've been all grown over.

But I wouldn't leave Nan by herself with angry Pa. And I

couldn't take her, could I? – she wouldn't go. If I even asked, she'd come over all funked. She might hate Pa worse even than I do, but he's chewed her away so badly, there's not enough left of her even to flee.

Anyway, what happens to those children? No one knows whether it's good or bad. You never hear, do you, of even so much as their bones being found. Maybe they do get to go somewhere, somewhere better, somewhere they can't find by themselves, but only with angels assisting.

Or maybe the angels eat them whole.

The first peaks tower over me, and the scrub is turning into fern-trees and mosses. The ground squeezes out water at every step. The air's cold and damp on my face, and smells of stone and water, not of greenery any more. We rarely come as far as this in our hunting.

It's changed everything, Nan being sick. She grows smaller and greyer-looking every time I glance at her. I'm scared to glance nowadays; my eyes and my worry might themselves suck the life out of her, the little that's left.

Of course, it's made Pa angrier. I can cook some of Nan's foods, but not like she can; I can keep the house in a sort of a way, but I'll always leave a broom where it can be tripped on, or let a mat get rain-soaked and ruined, or something else worth roaring at. At least when Pa's roaring at me he's not roaring at Nan, asking where's this and where's that, and how you boil a spud, and why all her type of work has to be done in such a fiddling complicated way, and just . . . wearing the woman away with his cataract of a voice, until she's bare more than a shadow in the bed, until she can speak nothing like words any more. Up to a day ago, she'd take a tiny sip of food from me, if he were outside the house and not likely to barge in and start raging, and if I talked her up to it. I'd tell her it were me that needed her, not to worry about Pa, just to get a bit weller for her poor grandson that she brought up from a baby. Not to leave *me* alone with the old bastard.

Fog pours across the moon, wraps me in cold. The gorge opens up, and now there's the never-ending noise and pother of the fresh-born river, where before was a crackless wall of silence.

The path turns into a steep, slippery ledge along the gorge wall, hardly wider than my foot in some places. The river bashes at the cliff's feet below – hard enough, you'd think, to shake me off my perch.

'So I'm here,' I pant, hand-over-handing, foot-over-footing along the wall, trying not to think how the weight of the cheese tucked in my shirt might drag me down to a pounding in the river. 'Whereabouts do the blamed things live? Where's their cave or crag?'

There'll be that wider space ahead, where Nan and Pa and I went that summer, in the days when Pa let Nan walk places instead of hiding her in the house. I remember it as being far, far up the gorge, a terrifying long way in, but now I round a shoulder of rock and there it is, a shallow sloping platform where the three of us might all stand if we pressed close, an angel would never fit there alongside. With my back to the rock, I try to breathe, in the thunder of the falls, in the water-smoke churning across my face, running cold into my neck.

At high summer, the falls were a narrow skein, lacquering the rocks, and Pa dived into a blue-green pool that was lined with rounded stones. Fish and fish-hunting birds darted there. Now, there's only noise and wind and black wetness, with the moon sharpening out of it and blurring back away.

'Angels!' I cry. All this water damps my voice; I might be shouting in the hayshed. 'Angels, come down! Someone needs you!'

Are they asleep, that they need to be woken? Are they near or far? How long and loud do I need shout?

'It's my nan! Come down and fix her! I have this cheese!' I continue, and so on. The falls roar. The mist catches my throat, presses my face. I feel like a mad person, bellowing alone in the night.

I feel so mad, in fact, that after some time I stop, my faith lost that anything can hear me, let alone follow my words. It's just another twist of Pa's temper, that he thought this could work, that angels would come 'cause *he* ordered them, and is used to his will being done. It's *so* cold here, and I'm soaked to the bone, and Nan is probably dead by now, without me there to comfort her at her last. And maybe that's why Pa sent me away, just to be cruel to her, cruel to us both, and make me miss her leaving.

I'm crouched in a ball when the thing plummets out of the mist, clattering. I shriek and spring open, banging my head on the rock. The smell hits me like a fistful of filthy hot sand.

'Mortal child,' says the angel. It's a reddish shadow in the mist, very tall, with a tremendous chest, no arms, and of course wings, like two sheaves of kindling-brush gathered in to its back. Its heat pushes me flat against the rock. Its eyes fix on me, red and rheumy as a drunk's, brainy as a priest's or showman's. Why would I *bother* a creature such as this, that can *fly*, for goodness' sake—

'Your offering?' Its voice is like a sheep-flock scattering in panic, the big ewes baying, the lambs squealing, all in the same sound.

'Oh!' I scrabble for the cheese. My fingers don't work very well. As I unwrap it, the paper pulls the belly-warmed cheese all out of shape. I step into the heat and lay the stretched, stuck mess on the ground, in the cloud of steam the red feet are raising from the wet rock.

The angel drops, props itself on its iron wing-claws and dips its head, like a gunney-bird into a corpse-cavity. With its teeth it shakes cheese and paper in two. It gulps down the first piece, moves springily to the second. Wrapping and all, that cheese, which Nan and Pa and I would have eked out over a week and maybe more, is gone, and the angel has swung to its feet, cheese-grease all up one cheek . . .

And now it's having some kind of fit of indigestion. Its throat rasps as if the cheese-paper is caught there, and it sways and stamps, its wings half-spread, swiping close to my face. Something is wrong with the cheese, or the paper, and the thing could unzip me with one of those claws, throat-to-thigh in a moment, for sickening it.

It retches twice, showing me the white ribs roofing its mouth. Its red-gold eyes weep and roll. Then it spits two bright, wet things, *thwap!*, *thwap!*, at my feet – yellow-hot pellets, sheathed in a thick jelly.

Harrumph! It wipes its mouth on its shoulder-mass. 'You were saying about your nan?' it hums.

'Huh?' Nan? I'd forgotten. Nan has never been smaller or greyer in my mind. 'I – I think she's dying,' I blurt. 'She's maybe dead by now.'

The angel looks at the moon. It stretches its face like a cat yawning – *eeagh*. 'Not quite. But soon. You'll need to walk fast, earth-mite. Redden your legs some. I'll precede you, ah?'

'Oh.' I have to think a bit to make sense of its noise. 'All right. You don't need – you know the way, then?'

The angel's eye-blazes sweep down to me. With a claw-tip it rolls the dimming gold pellets towards me, coating them with dirt.

'Oh – aye. Thank you—' It's like picking up warm turds. I put the slippery things in my trouser pocket. The front of my clothes is dry, the front of my hair, from the angel; steam tickles up the back of me, meeting a cold-sweat-dribble coming down.

The angel launches itself straight up. Its wings snap open, and its worm-root smell blasts out. Then I'm cold and damp and blind again, with the moon gone behind a cloud, and the water fighting to free its head in the gorge below.

It's nearly dawn. Pa's pacing up and down the fence like a penned puppy. When he sees me he makes a leap of frustration.

'It got here, then?' I call when he'll hear me.

'The blamed thing! Nobody said it'd— It's—' He's *gibbering* angry. 'It's sprayed all around the place with its bloody smell, that'll never go! It's mad as a cut-snake – You can't talk to it – It *sings*, like having your ears sawn off!' A rough braying starts up inside the house. 'Hear it!'

The windows and doorway glow orange. 'It'll be hot in there,' I say.

'All that firewood!' He's nearly weeping. Pa's fires are always mean and miserly; building a blaze like that is like gnawing direct on his heart. "Twould of seen us through *three winters*, husbanded right—'

'And Nan?'

He's angry again. 'Can I tell? Can I get near the woman for that *production* going on?' He follows me into the bright house. 'The damned creature—'

A stink like fireworks, a sound like accordions being bashed apart against trees, the fire blaring up the chimney. The angel squats on the table, working itself up to a crimson pitch. Veins seem to burst into sweat on its neck, running down, dripping off it. Its head clanks the lamp, which is turned up full as Pa would never have it. Bright yellow light and shadows of the lamp-case giddy about on the walls.

In the middle, Nan sprouts from the bed, her chopped hair all cockscombed from being lain on, the sheets like a swirl of mud around her hips. She has no colour of her own; she's angel-oranged pleats and bristles, against an orange wall. Even her eyes are oranged over, the pupils pinpricked to nothing.

I fight through the stenches to get to her, to make her lie down. But her body is stuck upright, all bands and wires. If I push her down, her knees will come up stiff, and we'll both be ridiculous.

I can't think with the din. I put my face in my hands, down on her kneebone through the grey sheets. My nan and pa

137

raised me to be useful, but there's nothing I can do here. This is like a big wind, a bad rain, where you just have to sit inside and hope that the roof holds, where you can do nothing 'til after, when it's clear what's damaged and what's gone altogether.

The lamp crashes to the table, cutting off the angel's roar. I start up, but the thing stops me with its clever red eyes, crushing the flames out of the spreading oil with its feet. Silence billows out with the burnt-leather smell; even the hearth-fire spouts up soundless; Pa's mouth makes anguished shouts at the door, but he's no noisier than a fiddle-string coiled and tied in its box.

And through the silence comes something immense and leisurely, that sheds the filth of the heavens from its dusty wings, to dim the hearth-fire, to lower the angel's greasy red lids over its eyes' intelligence, to bow down my pa in the doorway.

Whatever it is, it comes for all of us, ant or angel, lost child in the forest or lady and lord of manners. Tonight it's come for my nan, and it gathers her up out of the thing that was her self, up out of her own bones into its dark, dirty, soft, soft breast, unfisting her hands from the front of her nightshirt, laying down her remains, moving her on from us like a storm cloud dragging its rain.

Behind it, the night is suddenly vaster, colder, clearer. All the stars zing; the mountains glitter; towns and villages gather like bright mould in the valley-seams and along the coasts. Every movement in byre and bunny-hole, of leaf against leaf, of germ in soil and stream, turns and gleams and laminates every other, the whole world monstrously fancy, laced tight together, yet slopping over and unravelling in every direction, a grand brilliant wastage of the living and the dying.

Pa wakes me up – hours later, it must be. I'm curled on the bed around Nan's dead feet. The chill is back on the house, the fire a few red winkings in the hearth. Nothing is in its right place; I remember, I had some dreams that yammered and beat at the walls.

Pa has that dragged-through-a-bush look he gets when he drinks; his eyes could be weeping or just watery from the spirits. He yanks me off Nan, and hauls me outside. He flings me down in the yard-corner.

'Bury her *there*, that angel said,' he challenges me. 'So *dig*, boy.' He brings the spade, hurls it at me, lurches inside where he falls, and swears, and skitters something across the floor, and stays down.

I lie there a little while, listening to pig-snuffles and cow-plods. It's too early for birds; there's a low moon, strong stars.

Then I up and reach for the spade, because my stiff body needs to dig, because my nan needs to be in the ground, safe from Pa forever.

With the first bite of the spade into the earth, there's something different, juicier, lumpier than it should be. When I turn the soil, giant pearls fall out of it; some roll away; others, split by the blade, gleam white and wet in the star-light: tiny potatoes, no bigger than quail-eggs, thousands of them. They're grown so thickly, I have to not so much dig them as sift the soil out from among them with my hands. I eat one, and it crunches like wet stars, but tastes like sweet earth. It needs no salt or softening; it needs nothing but a mouth that's ready.

When I've dug out the whole crop, there's a Nan-sized hole, earth heaped to one side, a greater pile of potatoes to the other.

I step over snoring Pa, into his beaten house. I carry out the little that's left of my nan, the cloth of her stiffened with disuse. I lay her in the earth. I draw the bedsheet over not-her-face and bury her. I gather runners of grass, lay a cross-work of them over the grave and water them in well.

I'm hurrying now. I'll take not quite half the potatoes, in this sack. I'll wash before I go. I'll take this spare shirt of Pa's and the trousers—

I strip off at the pump. Something in the trouser-pocket makes a hard noise on the ground. Angel-pellets. They've stuck to the cloth; when I pull them free, they're brown, withered, and covered with pocket-litter. I lay them on the stone edge of the trough, and when I'm clean and dressed and booted, I take my knife and cut into one rubbery casing, to a harder core. I put my thumbs into the knife slit and pull it hard apart.

My knife has nicked the waist of a fat bean of gold. I roll it in my hand, feeling the weight, perhaps three coins worth. That'd pay us well for a whole year's cheeses. I think for a while, then slit the other pellet and place it open on the trough-rim. Let Pa find it, let a bird take it – I'm past caring, and I won't go back in that house.

I hoist my spud-sack onto my back. I leave the wreck of my pa on the floor, the husk of my nan in the ground. I get clear of Pa's shambling fences, and turn onto the road that leads down to the plain. The plain has towns and markets; it has smiths and shipwrights and mill-owners. A strong lad like me must be some earthly use to someone, down there, if he walks far enough.

perpetual light

Somewhere between here and Wagga, the winds were stirring up some metal. It took three 'Hellos?' before I even knew my mother was on the line.

'Just quietly overnight, it was. No alarm. The manager said she looked very peaceful; must've just gone quietly, no pain.'

Mum started telling me the funeral arrangements. I turned away from my project on the kitchen table and scribbled on the wall with near-dry marker.

'All the way out to Greville?' I said dismayed.

'It's what she wanted, Daphne. She arranged it all herself and it's paid for and done.'

'But Greville? There's nothing there! It's a ghost town, a filthy wasteland—'

'It's the town of your Gran's childhood, Daph, and she always meant to be buried there.'

'And so far . . .' Distance meant fuel; it meant money, which I didn't have . . .

'So I've organised a priest, and for that neighbour lady, Irini, to go out there with the body, and for the council to open the church, and for the hearse, and burial in the graveyard there. As I said, your Gran set it all up – all they needed was details of the date and time.'

And you did all this before you called me – but I didn't say that. Mum's family is wildly political. Put any three together, and two of them will start excluding the third. It was one of the things that drove my dad away. I'd made up my mind it was going to stop with me, that tradition.

I put down the phone feeling slightly sick. 'Nice timing, Gran,' I groaned. I sat down at the table. The power had been iffy for weeks, and everyone was using Gazlights, which gave a very bright light, but localised. The white WundaVerm packet, the seeds in their sachet, the planter tray, all gleamed on the shining table, but beyond was dimness.

I took out my cards and shuffled through them, but the circle was complete, hopelessly locked; I needed to inject some real cash to get it moving again.

I found my PalmPlot and went through my accounts. Forty-three cents in the cheque account, a big void in the Knowledge Nation account waiting for the next draught of scholarship. Petrol credits from Freedom's April Offer – they'd get me to Greville, but not back again. But the Old Girl badly needed a service, and from somewhere legitimate – the funeral was Thursday and I didn't have time to wait for Giglio to get spare time to do it.

I sighed. There'd been so many other times this year when I could've afforded Grandma dying – why couldn't she have done it then? It wasn't as if she'd even been properly alive, much of the last few years. I never want to get like that, lying like a slug in a bed, with nurses having to turn me and wash me and—

The Getaway account blinked up on my screen. Two thousand and four. If it went below two thousand, the transaction fees would send it straight into freefall. By the time the scholarship money came through I'd have lost another five hundred on top of the five hundred I'd need for the service and petrol. But the Getaway was my emergency account; I'd set it up just so I didn't have to borrow from friends when this kind of thing hit.

'Not happy, Gran,' I said, prodding the screen to make the transfer. I clicked off the 'Plot and took the Gaz into the front room to hunt down Statner's friend's number, the guy who knew everything about plants.

'Then you cover the seeds with the germinating medium, and Bob's your uncle.'

'I'm sorry?'

'And that's it,' said Statner's friend – from inside a blizzard, it sounded like. 'Then you wait. And if nothing comes up in two weeks, you got dudded on the seeds. Which happens a lot, so don't be put off.'

'Well, they weren't exactly cheap . . .' And I wasn't exactly in a position to buy fresh ones whenever I felt like it.

There was a little tantrum of static. '. . . worry, after a while you develop a feeling for viable ones. And their purveyors.'

'And then – if they *are* viable – it's just a matter of keeping the water up to them?'

'And the mixture, in the doses I told you. Listen, I've got to head off. Got to meet my mole from the Commonwealth

Nutri-domes. Say hi to Statner for me, okay? And thank him. Always good to find a new recruit.'

'I'll do that. Thanks for your help.'

The furry rushing sound of the open line collapsed into a clean dead beeping. I put down the phone and picked up the scissors. I snipped open the sachet. The seeds inside were like dried peas, lifeless and unpromising. Then I sliced through the WundaVerm's thick plastic. The stuff looked like white gravel with sequins stirred through. I wished I had music to steady my hand through this. But my sound system had gone bung a week ago, and it'd be another six weeks now until I could afford to fix it. I washed my hands with AntiBacto and got started.

'I don't like the idea at all,' said Nerida the Naturopath. 'Especially after that flu.'

'I know, but it's not as if I've got a choice. She's the only grandmother I knew properly. I'm her only grandchild.'

Nerida gave a defeated sigh. Sometimes I hated to think what a disappointing place the world must be to this woman. 'Well, you know what I'm here for: the whole organism. I can see that if you don't do this, you'll self-flagellate until you're sick. So just go. Go, and we'll do some serious stripping out of toxins when you get back. You've got your injections organised?'

'I go there straight after this.'

She made a releasing movement with her hands. 'Just be careful, is all I ask. Don't lose sight of the precautions in any moment of emotion. Your car's sealed okay?'

'It's pretty good.'

She glowered at me. 'Daphne, I *know* the kinds of vehicles you students drive.'

'This one is all right in the seals department. And it's just been serviced. I spent *three hundred* on the Old Girl.' Ah, the pain.

She waved me away. 'Go. Do what you have to do.'

The snippet behind the doctor's counter was very full of herself this morning. 'I'm sorry. Compassionate Allowance doesn't cover excursions for *grandparents'* funerals.'

I'd dealt with her before, though. 'I spoke to Inge McCormack at the Department. I have a case number. She said it would be all right.' I held out the number.

She didn't take it. 'The rule's very clear on this,' she scolded. 'If we start making exceptions—'

I reached over and stuck the note to her phone-base. 'You talk to Ms McCormack about exceptions. I've already had this argument.' I sat down and started leafing through the latest *Celebrity Plus*. She made the call; she made a fuss, went silent, tut-tutted, caved in. She banged around with her keyboard and files, sighing a lot. I paged through Anorexia Chic and Parched-Blueberry Crumble, listening to the snippet and feeling pleased with myself.

It wasn't so great walking out of there, though; I felt as if they'd sewn a golf ball into my bum-cheek. I'd have to sit on it all the way to Greville.

Your suspension needs looking at, the bloke at Artisan Autos had said.

How much's worth of looking? I'd asked straight away. He

told me and I nearly swooned. *Will it get me to Greville and back as it is?*

He sniffed. *Depends. If you're careful. Corrugations should be all right, but you don't want to hit any big potholes at speed.*

That's okay. I can be careful, I said, breathing again.

So here I was, driving out onto the pre-dawn Treeless Plain. The road ahead seemed to be steaming in the headlights' beams, the way the dust blew around on it. Flurries of the stuff hissed into the windscreen. It'd be *hiss* and *fwump* for a few hundred kilometres.

The seed tray was under the passenger seat, with my dad's olden-days textbooks fore and aft holding it steady. I didn't want to miss anything. And I didn't know anyone who'd mind them in the right spirit. And they were extra incentive to drive gently.

I clicked Overdrive on and puffed out relief. I had a functional car, safe seed tray, bloodstream swimming with antibodies. All I had to do now was stay awake and keep the Old Girl pointed in the right direction.

'What's he brought us tonight?' said Grandma, pulling back from stirring the fire. 'Another whirlygig?'

Blacktaw trotted to her, wearing his mad outdoor look. The creature in his mouth rowed a white leg in the air.

'Set it down, Taw-taw,' said Grandma. 'Set it free, now.' Blacktaw sat and looked doubtful. 'No pats until you do, I tell you!' I loved her haughty look.

Blacktaw lowered his head abjectly.

'That's right – put it down, Taw,' I said, trying to sound as sure as Grandma. The cat paused and checked with Grandma again.

'Come along, puss. Show me your night's work.'

Finally, he bobbed forward, put it down and sat back.

Every night Taw brought in something different. Mostly they were only broken inside, with their outer layers still bright and their remaining movements natural. But sometimes he lost his head and ate half, and brought us the rest, the light gone out of their eyes and the mechs and bio-springs trailing. This one was possumish and shrewish – a jumper, but with its jumping mechanism cracked. It had red button-eyes and miniature chuffer-train breathing.

'I think he's got a broken back, Taw,' said Grandma.

I thought Taw looked apologetic, but maybe he was just waiting for Grandma's word to start eating.

I reached down and patted some of the cold night air out of his fur. He bore with me, looking at Grandma.

'Do you know what I think?' She took her thread-knife from the basket beside her, bent down and made a slit in the little animal's lower abdomen. 'See? I thought so.' With the knife-tip she pressed on a swollen pink sac inside, and a clean, wet, white egg appeared, no bigger than the end segment of my thumb. The animal moved its forepaws anxiously, voided its bowels of two tiny silver cog-wheels, and died.

'What is it, then?' Grandma looked at me with mock puzzlement – this I also loved. 'Is it a mouse? Or is it a bird, laying eggs? This place, it's full of mysteries. This pussycat brings us a new mystery every night. Don't you, puss?'

'I think he's hungry, Grandma.'

'*Is* he? *Are* you hungry, big black Taw-taw? There's a lot of you to feed, certainly.'

'You're teasing him! You always tell me not to do that!'

'I know. I am a cruel old woman. Go, Taw-taw. Take it away and eat it. It's good food.' And she nudged it with her toe.

Blacktaw picked the animal up by the head, laid it closer to the fire, and started to crack and crunch.

Place of Many Possums, the Aborigines used to call Greville. It was like a lot of towns I'd passed through already this morning, a dying collection of buildings like eye sockets and mumbling jaws, grey under a grey sky. Its public buildings had been repurposed to death, through phases of gentrification, hippie squat and serious poorhouse. The Old Girl skittered on the built-up grit at every intersection.

I saw the glint of Mum's flatbed cab down near the cemetery. She and my auntie had started out from the Wagga Mecho-dome last night. They liked to think they were tough old birds; they didn't mind getting out to pee in the poisonous dark, or switching off all but the ventilator and kipping in the vehicle. 'We've got a lot of old immunities,' Auntie Pruitt was always saying, dressing up a boast as an apology for my new-age feebleness. They'd be getting precious about relatives' headstones, and the Fleeting Nature of Life. Going down there to join them would only be painful for all three of us.

The church was intact, but nothing was happening there yet. I parked and switched off most of the Old Girl. Then I clambered into the back seat, unclipped the torch, shifted

Excision of Facial Nerves out of the way and eased out the seed tray.

Nothing yet. Lifeless as a Japanese gravel garden. *Then you wait*, Statner's friend had said, and like an idiot I hadn't asked how long. It was three days now. I had no idea – should I be ditching the mixture already, or not bothering to look for another week and a half? I wished I were an olden-days person who just knew these things, who had this knowledge all through them that they'd just *osmosed* from their elders. Who knew how the world worked – big intricate animal that it was – instead of paying her heart out for instruction on a small electronic part of it, all the while praying that the economy would hold still long enough for the risk to be worth it.

A car was approaching. I clicked off the torch and slid the seeds and books away. The square afterimage of the torchlit tray hovered in my eyes.

It wasn't Mum and Auntie. It was the priest in his Lambda, a glossy black bit of ecclesiastical luxury. He stayed in the car, like me, except he probably had a fully functional sound system pumping out Gregorian chant. Or motivational talk, because he looked *young*, I noticed with disgust. One of those new wave gay married priests, probably. Not what Grandma would have wanted at all.

The flatbed scooted past me and around into the carpark on the far side of the church. I got out of the Old Girl, whanged her closed and strode around the church hands in pockets, meshing my eyelashes against the blowing grit.

Mum was just coming around the flatbed, and Pruitt was flinging herself out of the passenger seat. They both gave me the same hostile look, from deep within sisterdom. They were eerily the same: the big glasses, the mannish faces, the long harsh-blonded hair snaking out in the wind, the blue-and-white quilted flannel shirts. Both of them were wept dry and feeling old; part of the hostility was the hatred of old for young, however modern and allergic she might be.

It was very cold. The sky was a flat, bright, migraine-inducing grey. My eyes were already stinging.

'Come now, wake, child. It's a good morning for it.'

Blearily I peered over the quilt edge.

'Up you get,' said Grandma. 'We're going down to the creek, remember?'

'Oh, that's right!' I pushed back the heavy cotton sheet, the soft quilt.

I dressed quickly and warmly, and came out to her pulling on my mittens. Even inside, our breaths were misting on the air.

'Good girl,' said Grandma, and we went out of the cottage.

The forest was unfamiliar in the fog. I was wrapped in captured bed-warmth, but the cold nipped my nose and cheeks. The path wound down the hill through the trees. Bark wept off the tree trunks, staining the creamy plush under-skin rust and black. The pointy leaves dangled out of the mist. The cold air smelt of the medicine in them. Grandma had made this path; her flower beds, edged with scallop shells, showed vague in the mist ahead, brightened to pink and mauve and gold for the moments we passed them, and faded back to grey behind us.

We came to the place. It was away from the path, through

some dripping scrub. First Grandma's cardigan-back got dia-
mantéed, and then black-polka-dotted, with water shaken
from the leaves.

'I'm going to make a seat down here,' she whispered as we
settled on the leaf-matted ground. 'It'll be concrete, but made
to look like wood. Like a wooden plank propped on two tree
trunks. I've seen it done; it's very effective. Now shhh.' She
cocked her head towards where I should look, a little clearing
walled with dew-coated white stalks.

We quieted down to the silence of everything else. A few
bird-calls echoed as if in a vast empty room. The cold air
smelled of water and bruised leaves. Beside us the creek was a
cable of glass under a twisted roll of mist; it looked as if the
water were only trembling slightly, not actually flowing.

Grandma nudged me.

There was movement in the clearing, a fine net of rustling,
but no shape yet. When had he flown in? Or walked? Or
begun to shake together into being?

Then I saw where the net began and ended, and the bird
behind it, blurred and shadowed. He was a modest thing, neat
and busy in the grey morning. He would have been nothing
without the tail – no crown, no colour, nothing special.

He walked about arranging. He tidied leaves off his patch.
He pulled grasses into line. He fussed and fussed with one of
Grandma's garden shells, moving it about, getting it in the
right place, changing his mind.

Even with the tail, colour was not the thing. Two red-
brown feathers held the design together at either edge, and
the space between them was all muted sparkle, silver and
grey, with a froth of red-brown and cream at the very end. He

carried this fabulous artefact around with him while he did his housekeeping, and yet it was clean and bright, with no stray leaf or bush-bit caught up in it, with no part of it draggled or damp.

He went all around his patch, calling, waiting, moving the shell irritably, calling again. *Pi-ipe, pip*, he called. Rustle, scrape. *Py-eep, pip. Py-eep, pip.*

When the girl-bird came, she was nothing. She had no tail, and was a dull green. She said nothing, either, but he knew she was there, propped sideways with her claws in a tree, pretending not to see him.

And then, didn't he dance! He tipped his tail up and over his head, drawing and shivering it along the ground, watching her from within. The sound was feathers, but also metal — very light rich rustly metal. And all the while he made such noises! Bird noises and dog noises, train noises, noises of Grandma and me, calling in the cottage yard. Everything that went on, in and around here, this bird had heard and recorded, and now he was telling her the whole story.

The girl-bird came down out of the tree. She got busy at one side, pretending to look for food, and then she stepped casually onto the dance-floor, as if she'd just happened by.

He was thrilled. The noises stopped, and the tail shone and shook and spread, and dipped this way and that. He was trying so hard, my throat opened and closed in little silent moans of effort for him.

Fl'hup!, and she was gone. His tail swiftly folded and he was after her.

We listened for a few minutes. The bush had come alive

with the beginnings of a breeze, and leaves tinkled down from the invisible heights.

Then Grandma looked at me. 'A good show, yes?'

In the church the neighbour, Irini, was keeping vigil. I'd heard about but never met her; here she was, yellow-skinned, glossy dark-haired and martyred-looking. She sat to one side of the four candles in their square; among them, my Grandma was swaddled in knotted crimson synthetic bands, with a small cream-coloured mask inset. As I sat myself next to my mother in the first-but-one pew, I realised with a shock that this mask was Grandma's face, sculpted by God and by genes, shrunken to doll-likeness by time. *How she's shrunken!* I nearly whispered to Mum, until I saw her spotted hand in the clutches of Auntie Pruitt's.

The priest when he came in was offensively padded and protected. His electronics and goggles gave him a manufactured and unreadable face. He was athletic and young; he moved as if he'd never lost anyone, never known ill-health in any form.

The church itself was long uncleaned, only opened for this small occasion and no effort made for it. *No flowers*, Mum had said, so there were only cold, flat cheques sent to one of Grandma's charities (not from me – I couldn't afford that, though I might have afforded flowers), and here, on the day, saints with chipped noses shedding blessing on us from their grimy fingers. The priest's words were tinny and indistinct through his filter, and I sat after a while and watched the patterns the grit made, eddying around the floor, watched the nose-point of Grandma's little pinched face, so white.

Mother and Auntie Pruitt clutched to each other very hard and subdued. Did they go shopping especially for those matching outfits? I became preoccupied with glancing at them undetected, picking the differences in the cargo pants (it was in the tabs and the pocket placement) and the shirts (Pruitt's tartan had a thread of gold, my mother's was plain and more pilled).

'Eternal *sumth* grant unto her, oh *loggdg* . . .' squeaked the priest with bossy finality.

'And let perpetual light shine upon her,' we murmured.

Irini blew her nose, loudly. I was blinking a lot by now against the stinging in my eyes, and the skin under my arms, behind my knees, inside my elbows, was beginning to feel fat and welty and irritated. Grandma lay like a bound stone, radiating some kind of meaning I wouldn't be able to appreciate today. I was too itchy and angry and ill.

And then it was over, the whole dull, music-free, flowerless affair. The four of us – Irini, me, Mum and Pruitt – each took the end of a swaddling-band, and we carried Grandma out after the priest. He walked slightly too fast, but we let him go rocketing off. Grandma followed slowly, evenly, floatingly along like an airship, like a seriously injured body, properly cradled.

We laid her on the footpath outside the church gate. Blown twigs, grit and old dark brown dead leaves brought the pavement alive, around her utter stillness. The hearse, a grey banger from the days of the Epidemics, slid up to the kerb.

Mum and Auntie Pruitt stood back, shirts flapping, loose hair lashing about, faces red-mottled with the wind and with weeping. Irini was neater, her hair tucked up under a firmly pinned hat, a folded hankie pressed to her nose. She was the only one of us in skirt and stockings; she would pay for that tomorrow – didn't she know how much cortisone cream was? And she'd get no Compassionate Allowance, not being related *at all*.

'I can't quite believe it,' Mum wobbled, and Pruitt took her elbow in both hands, and looked intense. Grandma's face was already grit-speckled, and leaves were caught in the swaddling. If we left her there a little while, she would bury herself.

Irini performed the final part for all of us: stepped forward, knelt on the pavement and, holding her skirt decent in the wind, bent and kissed Grandma's forehead. It seemed only right – she was the one who knew Grandma best, these last days. It's the role of daughters to move ever away from their mothers (and could there be greater distance than between those two sighing snaky-haired lumberjacks of women and this close-wrapped, completed object at our feet?) and it's likely, isn't it, that someone will step in, and appreciate everything the daughters can't, being so busy pushing themselves out into the world, saying, *No, no, I'm not you.*

The priest said his few words to Mum and Auntie, stranger to strangers. He was in the Lambda before you could say *condolences*. He drew away slowly, but you could hear the relief in the engine revs as he rounded the corner onto the highway.

We were walking back from a day at the lake, toiling slowly along the dirt road up the last long rise to Grandma's turn-off. In a few more steps the late sun would be blazing in our eyes –

the rise was topped with a pink-gold fur of grass; the road cut a bright, straggling hole through the slim black trees.

Into that arbour a man strolled, up from the far side of the rise. I thought he was wearing a plumed costume. I wasn't surprised; I wouldn't have been surprised at anything that walked out of the landscape at Grandma's – the place was full of wonders. But as he came down the hill I saw that he was quite an ordinary man. His hat was a beloved worn hat, grown fast to his head, but his boilersuit and boots were the dark-blue Meeko-system standard.

At his waist he wore a special belt with quantities of bunched feathers strung along it, swinging. The sunlight behind him filled the bunches with needles of light, and made the main curves shine like polished blades, and glowed in the frothier feathers. That delicious rustling, of soft live metal, whispered at us as he neared us.

'Good evening to you!' Grandma said in her uphill voice.

'Evening.'

Grandma stopped. 'Do you have birds there, or only feathers?'

'Oh no, I've got whole birds,' He lifted an armful of glitter. The small grey bodies hung beneath. Some were undamaged; others were part-devoured or crushed, the feathers matted with oil or blood; one was just the root of the tail, with the fine metal leg structure, the kera-plas claw-tips stripped of their paint.

I wanted to reach in and touch, make the leg bend with my finger, but I sensed Grandma's silence. She had drawn back in the stiffest disapproval, her whiskery mouth pursed. 'The child doesn't need to see that,' she said sharply.

The man dropped the tails over the bodies, and smiled down at me. 'They can get pretty banged up, out here in the bush. Every so often we go round and collect 'em all up, make 'em pretty again, and put them back out all fresh.'

Grandma drew in her breath to speak, but he said to her, 'I've always believed in giving it to 'em straight, little kids.'

'Well!'

'Yeah. Best to let 'em see things as they are. They can take it.'

'Oh, you *think* so,' said Grandma.

He winked at me and walked on past us, down the road, his flounced bird-skirt setting up its fine rustling. I turned to watch him.

'Come along, Daphne,' said Grandma up ahead.

I caught up with her and we topped the hill into the full orange blast of the sunset.

'Those people aren't meant to be *seen*,' she puffed. 'Not by residents, not once induction's complete. I shall write a letter to management.'

'Why? What would management do?'

'Put him in his place, I hope. Out of sight.'

I looked back down the hill. He already was out of sight. The white road was empty, slipping away into the dusky bush.

'That cloud's thickening,' said Irini, peering out the Old Girl's windscreen.

I didn't answer. I felt ratty. Mum and Pruitt together always made me feel ratty, even without Greville's pollutants and my usual overreaction to the injections. And now I had to ferry

Irini home. Mum and Pruitt had only paid to *bring* Grandma to Greville. They hadn't bought Irini a return trip.

Well, we knew you'd be going that way anyway, darling, said Pruitt.

It just would've been nice for someone to tell me, I'd muttered. *Ahead of time.*

You'll be fine. She's a nice old thing.

Pruitt was already light on her feet anticipating the trip home, the music, the *communing*. They spoke their own language together, those two. They might look like sides of beef, but they gushed at each other like Victorian spinster poets. If we'd all lived in the same town, and all come out together as a funeral party should – as blood relations, most of us – I'd be throwing up by now, having listened to that all the way.

As it was, my eyes were swelling and my nose was bunged up, and I had a lot of blowing to do and a few pills to take when I got into the Old Girl. Then, 'That cloud's thickening,' said Irini, and soon we were flying down the highway through the middle of the grey blow.

I did talk with Irini – about Grandma's sweetness in her old age, about how frequently she reminisced about her time with me in the Meeko-system, about how the world has changed, about how death takes all of us one way or another – that hasn't changed, we haven't managed to mess up that system, have we! When her talk faded and her head began to loll, I pulled over, inflated the travel pillow and settled it round her neck. 'Oh thank you, dear,' she murmured from inside a fraying dream. 'Very kind.'

It was lonelier than driving alone, driving sleeping-Irini. It was midafternoon, but I had to switch the headlights on to find the road. It was like driving down the eye of a tornado, its rings shifting over us, charcoal, dirty cream, mid-grey. The Old Girl's seals weren't great, despite what I'd told Nerida. The finer dust was filtering in, powdering Irini's navy skirt, tickling my sensitive nose. Nerida would have me on the Brassica drops for months after this. Under Irini's seat, the WundaVerm would be speckled black. Would toxins leach into the mixture and kill off the plants before they started? Or would I drop Irini off, and toil home, and take the tray inside, and put it under the Gazlight, and see, just like in the old documentaries, the first pearly stalk unbend its elbow, wander lightwards, and spread its small green hand? Would they all twelve prove viable, their stalks strengthening, their greenness emerging, thickening, bunching, seemingly out of nothing and for no reason, vibrating slightly in their rows?

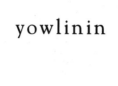

yowlinin

I wouldn't say Harrow's son was handsome – not handsome that people would notice. He's got a handsomeness that only I can see, so only I watch him. Even he himself doesn't know about it yet, so he doesn't preen, like some of the finer town-kids do.

He's right below me, skinning munkees. With their fur peeled off, they look like shiny wet people, but longer and thinner. And smaller, of course. He hooks the peeled ones over a branch-stump, lower down my tree. There are too many for him and his dad to use; they must be going to market.

I could reach down and touch his scumbly hair, with the little bits dried and goldened by the summer. That would freak him, wouldn't it? – well and truly. One second he's quickly slitting munkee-skin, the next he's eye to eye with nutty me, as good as touched by yowlinins himself. I wouldn't do that to him. Heck, I wouldn't do that to *me*. Where would I come, these long days? How would I pass my time?

He's grumbling under his breath; none of these kids knows how good they've got it. A dad to order you around (a mam, too, most of them); school to go to; a house to provide for; a plough to pull to save your old man's plough-busted back. Days made, hours filled – to have a duty is a wonderful thing. They should try going without for a week or two; they'd scuttle back to whisk-brooming and munkee-cleaning fast enough. These kids don't know how long a day can be.

He goes off to get a sack. The munkees hang there as if they expect a spanking, their skinny backs pink, veined purple. I could pinch one (they make a good pot), but I don't do that kind of thing now. It's weird, how my days of mischief just ended. Except, only I know they did; everyone else still thinks I'm out for trouble, whatever I do. I get shooed off places I never even bothered when I *was* bad.

Skit, girl, skit you! Get your yowlinin-paws off my stall!

But I'm not! I'm only looking—

Get gone. No one buys when you're hanging around like a smell.

Here he comes. My, he looks cross, funny boy. Puts away the munkees and ties the bag. He's got nice hands that know what they're doing. Man hands, but on a boy body. Takes away the sack, comes back, takes the skins off to the house for stretching.

Now it's quiet, but for flies zooming to the drops of munkee-blood. Well, that was good, a good long look. I won't get another like that for a while. I turn over and lounge along the branch. Through the leaves there's a sky bright as scrubbed blue-ware. There's enough wind for his dad's corn crop to go shushing, shushing, like a mam over her babies when yowlinins is loose.

I lie there until they go, with their little handcart of

early-corn and munkees. I could go in their house; the dog knows me, and lets me. But there'd be nothing new – I was only there a little while ago. I've got the smell of him in my memory and I don't need to lie on his bed to call it up.

I get down and cut through the corn, to the road. I sit among the stalks, a little way in, so I don't show, I wait and watch.

Here they come. This is the way the world will see him; look how his frown goes and he straightens, as he gets closer to town. If I were a town-girl, his spirit might be lifting for me. I did dream that, once. But when I woke up I was the old touched, unlucky one again, hardly better than munkee myself.

I wait a while and then follow them up the road, keeping where they can't see me. Must be a storm coming; the corn-sparrows is down hopping among the stalks, instead of up on top taking grain out of the cob-ends. I look all around the edges of the polished sky. Nothing yet.

Market's starting to buzz when I get there. I go up on the steps of the cornstore and settle; I figure if they see me *not* making mischief long enough . . . *Well, what will happen? They will welcome me as bosom-family?* Maybe not that. Maybe they'll just stop skitting me whenever I come near. But it takes luckies a while to notice things.

I'm in the sun, but the sun is not quite warm. Usually I get dozy here, but today there's a tickling breeze, smelling of the faraway sea. I went there once, though no one here believes me.

It's true. Bigger than yowlinins, and all along the shore, there's this wild-water, crashing and crashing. It's like madness to stay there—

169

Yeah, and you'd know that. They touched you in the head, didn't they? The kids were hanging along the schoolyard fence, kicking the low-rail.

Touched her all over, I heard, says another with a dirty laugh.

I tell you, even your head couldn't hold such noise, such size of water. On and on to a flat line of nowhere, all boiling! I was full of it. I'd been sure they'd want to hear; I know better now. Lucky people don't want news. They want to know that things are the same – that they're still lucky, hey.

Anyway, I did go. *I* know what the sea looks like. And smells like: like this, that I can smell now, salt and rubber-weed on the air, and as if it'd be easier the second time, to stand in the sandhills and watch those water-beasts fighting and falling into the beach. It's a bit magic, the sea, I think; puts its call in you, and forever after it can tweak you by the nose, by that smell, any time.

Can't understand why it's so busy here today, everyone out and milling like ants readying for rain. People lean at the frippery stall, fingering the blue-ware figurines; everyone does loud chat with the goat-man and the corn-wives and the donkey-carter. I listen in for gossip, but it's nothing; gloomy weather-talk, crop-talk, babies and marriages and money. No one's in a hurry to go home. There are a lot of families around who should be in fields cutting corn; it's best to get in what crop you can, as it comes good, so you've got plenty stored against storm or monster. If I'd my land, that was my mam and dad's, that's what I'd be doing. But I was too young when they were tooken, and the land went into the rent-box, and now is fallow under Goodman Thatcher.

I sniff the sea-ish air and look around for my boy. His dad is settled with the other old men, two steps below me. Harrowson will be dealing at the cornstore, or even already – ah, there! – standing by the butcher, keeping the flies off the show-munkee propped over the sack. By the size of the sack, he's already sold a couple. I can read his lips, even hear him a little: *Trap-munkees, good and fresh! Pot these up with garlic-root and taters and they're good as hutch-rabbit. Tasty trap-munkees, fresh as fresh!*

I must have had hutch-rabbit once, but I wouldn't remember. Now, *wild*-rabbit I know well – nasty little beasts made of string. But better than nothing when you've wandered a way from the town.

Then something happens under my eyes that makes me forget my love-boy, makes me forget just about everything I know.

It looks like a stone, a smooth, biscuity-coloured stone, the size of my thumbnail, on the step next to my foot. It starts rocking, all by itself, jerkily. I stare at it. I draw my knife and steady the stone with the point. I can feel in the handle just a very small squirm, from *inside the stone*. I'm still not scared, even seeing the tiny split happen along the side; I've seen so many different things hatch, from your ordinary cackle-bird to those frog babies that pop out of their mams' backs in Fenny Brook. The beetle inside it pushes the shell apart, and even then I admire it, so round-backed and shiny, with red or green wing-cases depending on which way it catches the light. Pretty as jewellery.

Then I see the short black sucking-tube of its face. I paw the nearest shoulder.

It's my boy's dad. 'Hands off me, yowlinin-toy, left-behind.'

He shrugs away from me, but he must see my horrified face, and he looks down, and he has one glimpse of the jewel-drop of beetle before it hoists up its skirts and flies *thrrrrrr!* up away between us.

'What was that?' he says to me, although he knows.

'They're coming again.' Such small words, and I say them so softly.

I would give my knife and the arm that holds it to have him spit on me, or laugh, or rouse at me. Or just turn away and settle back to corn-talk with the other men. But his face – well, mine must look the same, all eyes and nostrils. And he gets down backwards off the steps, and backs into the market. His eyes keep coming to mine; *we saw what we saw, didn't we?*, we ask each other, and the sight of each other asking is our answer.

He pushes through to his son, and tries to drag him away by the arm. The boy puts up a fight – *What about all these good munkees?* To get him moving the dad says, *All right, bring them*, and the boy gathers them up, angry and puzzled. He tries to follow his dad's last fearful glance at me, but he's not used to seeing me, not used to noticing; he's still searching the faces on the cornstore steps as his dad hurries him out of the square to where the carts are minded.

Maybe none of that just happened. The chat goes on, the swap of coin and goods, the fingering of fruit, the eyeing of meat. But now there's a beetle-case broken on the step. Over everything, the sky, clean of even a skerrick of cloud, is like a person looking away and whistling.

I pick up the beetle-case and stand up on my step. 'Hey! Listen!' My voice sounds mad and shrill, even to me. I hold up the evidence. 'I just saw a dormer-beetle hatching! Here, see? Right here on this step!'

A chill goes out through the crowd; a quietness opens for me to shout it out again. 'A dormer-beetle. You know what that means!' I look out at all their eyes. A few people leave straight away – why don't they all? You've got to spread out wide for yowlinins – you gather, they head for the clump, and take every one of you.

A fruit-lady is first. 'You've got monsters on the brain, girl,' she says into the silence, and relieved laughs go up around her.

A mother with a baby: 'How dare you try such trouble! How dare you put a scare on us!'

'She's touched, that's all,' says one of the mayor's men.

'I've got the case here! I saw it with my own eyes! So did Goodman Harrow – he was right here talking with you old ones, only a moment ago, and now he's fled! He took his son, that was selling munkees – do you see either of them now?'

That brings an even horribler silence. One of the old men totters upright. 'Show me the case, girl. A dormer-beetle is very like a ruby-beetle.'

'Yes, it could easily be a mistake,' says the fruit-lady.

I check my memory. 'No, there was green on it. And I saw the snout. *Harrow* saw, and he fled – you'd believe him, wouldn't you?'

'Maybe, if he were here to speak.'

'I wouldn't credit anything that drunkard has to say.'

Now the old man has finished examining the case, and he takes a step up, leaning on his stick. I see his smirking face and my heart sinks.

'It's a ruby, all right,' he cries, handing the pieces back to me.

People cheer and clap. I look into his eyes and see how pleased he is to have bettered me.

'He's blind!' I shout. 'I saw the wings, green and red. I tell you, he wouldn't see his own poke-pole if it reared up at midday! Harrow's gone, Harrow's putting up shutters and burying coin. That's what all of you should be doing—'

But smack! The frippery-woman is at me from the side. She wallops my head and drags me off by the ear – to cheers and laughter.

'Have you outlawed, I will!' she hisses into my face. 'I had a pearl necklace I've been trying to shed for months! Right up against the lady's neck, it was, and her reaching for her purse, when you—' She gives me another thump and a shake. 'You freak her with this monster-talk, this trickery. And now she's gone, and months again before another likely buyer comes through here.'

''S not trickery,' I manage.

'You're a thief and a savage, and you've never uttered a true word in your life – and now you've near ruined me, you scrawny scrag-end, and the mayor'll hear of it, don't you worry. I'll have you run out of town, you curse!' And she flings me in the wet-alley running by the cornstore, right on a pile of stink that clogs on my shoulder. And she's gone, but a bright-eyed bunch of market-kids is there with bad eggs and cabbage stalks to throw. I pick my way up the alley with all of that thumping into my back.

I get out of town. I'm wild, I can tell you, shaking with their stupidity and the terrible smells on me. And with straight fear, too. Do they forget, that the person who'd be most scared of yowlinins is me? How would someone who'd ever seen them, let alone been tossed about by them, tossed aside for the bigger meat of her dad and mam, ever make a *trick* of them? They just don't know; they're just too lucky.

The two halves of the beetle-case hurt my hand from being clutched so hard. I open it up. He's right, it is very like a ruby-beetle's. *But it had a snout. I saw it. To suck up the drool.*

I was hardly out of napkins back then. They found me playing with the dormers, patting the sheets of them gathered on the puddles, of drool plain and drool-and-blood mixed. (I heard all this over the schoolyard fence, and from Goodwoman Pratt who used to leave me food and rags on her back step, until her goodman beat her for it. All I remember is a huge woman bending down out of the sky, exclaiming.)

I'm hurrying, I don't know where. Nowhere's safe. Yowlinins come up anywhere, everywhere, and they roam too, and drool on everything – from their mouths, sure, but also from all their skin, which is like snails', green-grey, with froth on. They're big, tasselly things, so the drool sprays all over, and whatever they drool on you can't eat any more, even if it were the tiniest droplet. If they've thrown themselves across your cornfield, you can't count on much of your crop; if they've shooken about in your herd and it goes on a cow's tongue, or in its ear, that cow dies – and this ruin's on top of any *people* you might lose, if people you have, and if you don't get lost yourself.

I hurry across pasture towards the forest, thinking to get up high, to have some kind of view. Then I get a hideous feeling in my feet, like the ground can't be trusted. 'Aagh!' I shout, and go hopping across this herd-grass, watching the clumps of pea-bed daisies in case any should start to wobble. Part of me is interested that I know to do this, even if it is so long since yowlinins last came. (People always say, *They might not come ever again*, but older people always answer, *They might come tomorrow, too, so put away corn.*)

And then – like a bad dream, when your fear makes the feared thing happen – yes, a daisy clump *does* shake, and slowly uproot itself. I stop hopping, and stare to make sure it's not just my eyes making tricks, and then I run, and I'm shouting, too, because shouting helps me run faster, and anyway others are shouting and screaming, behind me, in town. I'm running for the only tree I can get to fast, Harrow's tree. There's just too much endless *field* between here and the forest! The ground – yow! – is starting to blip and bump up like thick, slow-boiling porridge. I seem to fly, running fast on my very toe-tips, and even when the first yowlinin blasts up out of Harrow's corn crop, so ghastly high in its shower of dirt and drool, I keep running, darting around it like it's only a tree itself, not a frothing monster, with a howling hunger in it.

I make the tree, uneaten, amazed, stupid with fright. I scramble up, into the middle, as if the flimsy leaves will protect me, as if the skinny branches will hold me safe. And I curl up like a baby, thinking, *How ever can I be so lucky again, as I was? Can a person be tossed aside twice in her life?* They've got teeth, I just saw, like long grey thorns, massed in their mouths. They would have picked me up in their teeth to toss me, last time – by a miracle they only holed my clothes, not my skin.

And now the teeth are everywhere, bursting up all over the country. The yowlinin cry is like a night cat's, spoiling for a fight, a terrible baleful rising drone, exploding to thuds and screeches. I can't think, only curl as tight as my muscles will pull me. I'm not even here – or I won't be, soon. Any moment now, out of their earth-shaking, out of that horrible wailing that bends your bones and won't shut up, one of them will come, one of them will find me, one of them will finish the job, good and proper.

Green leaves, heart-shaped, crowds of them. Their stalks are yellow, and the yellow strikes down the middle of each leaf and fans out into the green. On the smooth brown-red tree arm are oval spots, silver-grey like munkee fur. Through the leaves above me, that same shiny-dinnerplate sky. It all looks so fresh after the squished red-black of my eyelids. It's quiet and still; it has been for ages. A lifeless quiet, without a bird in it; no rustle of corn, no shift of beast in byre or field.

I slither a little lower. There's a yowlinin mud-hole over by Harrow's house, a scatter of munkee corpses. (They don't like munkee; you can't buy them off with munkee. *They won't be distracted*, says Goodwoman Pratt. *Won't be distracted and they won't be killed, 'less you take out both their eyes, clear and complete, and how you ever get close enough to do that I'd not know, for they never sleep over ground*). So Harrow and his son made it back, that means, if there are munkees here.

I'm in the lowest branches now. Oh, it's too quiet. Look at that stove-in roof. The yowlinin must've gone in after the smell of them. It's had a good rummage: munkee-skins on their frames all over the yard, the door broken out from all the stirring around inside, that dog in black and white pieces around the end of its chain. If they were in the house, it's got 'em. Dormer-beetles are everywhere, black and busy, winking red and green light. They're spattered all over the sustenance-garden along the side there, crusted on the drools on the house and shed. Patches of them mark a yowlinin's drag-path into the corn, where the thing, having fed, has gone to ground again, to sleep who knows how long.

Movement behind the house – I shrink up into the tree again. Off in the distance there's a yowl – there are always these outriders, after the main mass. I'll stay up here as long as I have to. It seems to be a safe place; I'm alive, aren't I? Though I can scarce believe it. And do I *want* to be alive, in such a dead world?

Movement again. It could be people, or it could be the bumpings of a yowlinin on the rise. I lie out thin along a branch, my heart banging again.

It's my boy. I nearly fall out of my tree. He stumbles from behind the house, over the spilled stone. He comes to the front, stares around, sees the dog pieces and goes to them. He starts putting them together, but his hands are shaking too badly to do much of a job, and he has to stop to cry. He's filthy, too, must've fallen in the mud-hole. Almost as filthy as me. If I didn't smell so bad I'd go down there so he wouldn't be all alone – me, either. Maybe I should go down anyway. Or maybe just call out from here. But I don't want to startle him. What if he chased me off? Could I bear that, just now?

Then bursts up the yowlinin, the one with my name on it. It's only a tree-trunk away from me, its head caught and fighting in the branches, gargling louder than thunder. Its great, flat, unlidded eyes loll – they're for seeing things underground, useless out here. A tassel of it slaps me wetly on the back of my head. Straight away come dormer-beetles, from all directions. Straight away the skin of my head and neck starts to pain like its stuffed full of needles.

'All right, then, beast,' yells Harrowson, 'come and get me! Don't make me a left-behind! Take every scrap of me!'

Idiot boy – this one's mine, doesn't he know?

The yowlinin yowls and lowers itself out of the tree-branches. Its breath wheezes among its teeth. It nods around for him, just below me.

'I'm over here, dolt!' yells Harrowson. He gets up from the dog. His face is red and mucky and teary and he doesn't know what he's doing. I gather to a crouch on the branch. 'What are you looking for? Eat me, here! A tasty mor-hor-horsel!' And he comes right up to the froth-draped front of it and starts pounding the soft bits. I jump.

A yowlinin's only got sort-of shoulders; the tops of the limb-y things that the tassels slop from. The only place to hold it is in its mouth corner, where the lip stretches and tightens against the teeth and holds my fingers without slipping. My other hand's cutting out the far eye, my knife feeling deep into the cone-shaped socket. My eyes are tight closed, and my mouth, against the poison gunk of the thing – my lips, my lids, my whole face and arms and legs are swarming with its stings.

I gave a little bit, even, says Goodwoman Pratt, *and the thing will go down again, and grow back, and come to rise another day.* So let it thrash, let it bellow and froth and shred leaves, let it whack me against branches behind; I will cut that tough, slippery eye-root down there in the point of the cone. I will keep scraping until the socket is clean. And then, because I'm sliding already, because my only steady place is my stinging maw-trapped fingers, I'll start the second – *Oof!* I am swimming in drool, spitting in terror of swallowing it, and only the knife itself is holding me here as it cuts to bone, solid bone in a world of squash and slither and foam.

I cut the second gristly eye-root through. The eye-cone falls out and knocks me swinging, and my fingers slip from the yawning mouth, and I drop to the ground as the yowlinin splinters the tree with its head, stuns itself with a blow that would have crushed me, killed me quicker than yowlinin-teeth.

Harrowson has dropped to the ground; he raves and weeps. Squinting through my gunked eyelashes, I take his ankle and pull him out of the beast's reach, for it's still half in the earth, not pulling itself free to roam. Wet grey fluff fountains from its eyes, and it lashes hugely back and forth, suffering. Glug is coming up through its teeth, too, and the yowling has gone gargly and choked-sounding.

Harrowson and me, we're well back from it, back from the squashed-snail stench. I'm feeling sicker and sicker, the worse the yowlinin flails, the harder it drowns. It's all mixed up with the pain flaming thick in my skin. I spit and spit, and still it feels as if gunk has slipped down my throat and burst and foamed inside me. It keeps foaming up the back of my nose.

Finally the yowlinin falls. Its falling pulls one stubby leg out of the mud. The rubbery toe-things grope a last grope. The beast rolls and arches once horribly, then slackens onto the ground.

The dormers come down in a thrumming cloud. They cloak the whole yowlinin-corpse, dark and glittering. They coat me, too, like perfect armour, while Harrowson's got spots, like decorations, where the yowlinin sprayed him, and his hands are in mittens, his front an apron, of dormers. He's weakly retching, lying face down where I dragged him, his forehead to the dust. Both of us are a-shiver with yowlinin-sickness.

'They got my dad,' he finally says.

I nod, and spit, and shiver more. 'Mm. M-mine, too.'

'He was just getting into the cess with me, and it came up behind.'

'You were in cess?'

'They don't smell you if you're in the shit. They think you're people's leavings, 'stead of people. My dad said. It worked for him last time. But he weren't quick enough. They throw you up, you know, like a dog throws a munkee.' He looks around at me with the awfulness of it. 'I saw him go up in the air, and he was still fighting, all the way—'

'Stop. I know all that.' *Her skirt flying, her hair falling free of its cloth. His tools spinning out of the pouch at his belt, in a curve across the sky – hammer, hasp-bother, and a spray of copper-bright tacks—*

'I saw him come down . . . and the thing—' Sobs shake him. He mouths, *snap*, and one of his mittens rises and snaps closed, sending dormers dizzying.

I turn away. I could sit down and mourn, as he mourns. That's one way to win a boy, to sit close and share miseries. I've watched that happen, from the schoolyard tree.

But I can't. My mourning time is long ago. That arc of dad

in the sky, that arc of mam, those are gone hard in the shape of me; they're not fresh-pressed and hurting like this boy's.

I leave him weeping, flat on the ground, and go down to the stream. I wash myself and my knife well, scrubbing us with sand to get all the gunk off. Already it's raised welts on me, numb on the surface, sore deeper down. But the gagging lessens as I pound my clothes and squeeze them out with my welted hands, and put them back on still damp.

I go back up, past Harrowson. He's quiet now, poor boy, but still flat under his dormer-blanket. In the house-mess I find the big pot, and drag it out and put it on the handcart. At the clang of it Harrowson sits up and dully watches. I don't look at him much, but my thoughts sit about him, small, fine, silent flames of hope.

Three of the munkees are beetle-free. I take them to the stream and rinse the dirt off them, and throw them into the pot. I go around to the garden, and in a clean corner I pull a carrot and some garlic and taters. I carry them back, brushing the soil off them. Harrowson is rising slowly to his feet, not knowing what to do, or what I'm doing.

'You go for a wash,' I say. 'In your stream, not your pond – you need running water for yowlinin-gunk. And then we'll go.'

'Huh?'

'Everyone brought what they had into town last time, Goodwife Pratt said, and fed each other, 'cause some didn't have anything. These munkees won't keep, for just you.'

He looks at the pot on the cart, and at me. And it was a mistake to get so clean and damp and ready. I should have just slipped away into the cornfield. For I know what's coming.

'Only . . .' He falters. He might not even say it.

But he does. 'Only, you come separate.' His eyes slide back to the pot. 'You come into town round by the piggeries or something, and maybe not exactly at the same time. You know?'

Ah yes, I know. Behind him, the dead yowlinin is piled gross and grey. One of its eye-cones has rolled in among the dog, and glistens there as a cone of dirt and beetles.

'I know, you saved me and everything,' he continues. However small he tries to make it sound, it won't *go* small. He knows it, and I know it, but he's still going to be one of them, a lucky village boy. He's not going to change. I put up my swollen hands, but he keeps on, though more softly. 'I'm old enough to claim my land,' he says. 'It's different for me.'

'Doesn't have to be.' The words come out all blunt and wild. Of course, it must be hard, having once been lucky. 'You can say it's different if you want, but the only difference is, you had your mum and dad longer. You were just a bit luckier, that's all, for a bit longer. But you still lost everything, and by those monsters. Just like me.'

Everything except your land and your place. Yes, it *is* different – he's right. Nothing I say will make him want me, make him prefer me to propertied girls, and familied ones.

'Never mind,' I say. I start walking, a long way around him. 'There's lots to eat out here, if you know where to find it.' As if I'm too good for his munkees – munkees are for soft people who can't handle wild-meat and bush-berries. As if my mouth wasn't watering for the beasts just a minute ago as I chopped.

183

What was I doing, thinking him handsome, calling him mine? Who did I think I was, all these months, following and watching him? This must be what they call love sickness. But the love has fallen from my eyes now, and left only the sickness.

'I'm sorry,' he says, but he's glad. He *is* sorry, but he's more glad. His feet stay still, but his body turns to watch me go, to see me off.

I'm not looking at him any more. I'm stepping over dog-chunk and beetle-patch, working around the yowlinin-corpse, to disappear into a clean part of the corn. And I'm the only one who can smell, through the dog-blood and the cess, through the sap, slime and splintered timber-rot, the thin sharp salt, on the breeze, of the sea.

◆

rite of spring

This wind doesn't shriek or moan – nothing so personal. When the river took Jinny Lempwick last spring and half-killed her while we watched, it was doing what the wind's doing now, racing so strongly that a little thing like a person was never going to matter. All I can do is keep myself out of the main force of it, because it doesn't know how to care.

It's madness to be here at all, up on Beard's Top in an end-of-winter blizzard – and I'm near mad. I'm past thinking about soup, about fire, about sleep; I can only gape at how dumb, what a stupid idea, who thought of this? My mitted hands grasp and fumble ice and rock in front of my eyes. How do they keep going? How do these legs keep pushing me up the mountain as if I believed, as if I were as mad as my mad mother, or my mad, holy brother? Don't they realise I'm not made of the same stuff?

I don't know how my scrawny brother managed last year, with this robe in his pack. I feel as if only my hunting, my built-up muscles and my good lungs, stop me toppling off into the darkness. Sappy little Florius is stronger than I thought. I knew Mum was strong; Mum's the kind of person who can move a strapping great hunter like Stock Cherrymeadow aside with a word, with the force of a single lifted eyebrow. If she were in good health she'd be laughing now, thinking of me up here. Hellfire, she'd be here herself, not letting a big brawnhead like me go about her important business.

But she's not in good health. Felled to her bed, our mum, coughing, and raging at the cough. 'Don't come near me, thick boy! Just stop still and listen for a change!' And between her instructions I could hear Florius trying to breathe, in the outer room by the fire. He sounded like a hog caught in a prickle-bush. It hurt just to listen. Mark Langhorne's lost all his five daughters to this cough.

Here we are, the cairn. This is where it all starts to happen. 'Don't get changed up top,' Mum said, 'or the wind'll snatch the robe away and we'll never afford another.' *And I'll not forgive you, ever,* she may as well have said, *and neither will anyone else in the village. Anything that goes wrong from here until king's-turn will be your fault and no one else's. May as well throw yourself off after the robe, for your life won't be worth living if you come back without it.*

So I use what small shelter the cairn gives to wrestle the robe out of the pack. The cold has stiffened it into great gold-crusted boards – I'm afraid it'll crack apart in my hands.

It's a wondrous treasure. I've only seen it the once, when Parson Pinknose shuffled in with it, autumn before last. 'It's all yours now, Ma'am,' he miseried. 'They won't let me do the thing again, after three summers' drouth.'

'Neither they should,' crabbed my mum. 'You Pinchnazes

always do sloppy work, for all your prating about tradition. Next time *your* lot breeds a Deep One, do us all a favour and let its cord strangle it.'

You could tell the parson was too low-feeling to fight her back as she liked. He sighed as he pulled open the cloth bag, and the robe – well, nothing like that had ever been in our house before. Like bagged-up dragon-fire, it was, all full of danger and brightness. It pulled me out of my corner as on a trap-loop.

'You keep your mitts off,' my mum said, smacking me away and pulling the drawstring tight. 'What do you think you're up to, Parson, opening that here?' She glared at him.

'Just a last look, I thought,' said Pinknose wetly.

'A look for every boy and his dog? You know that's only for the Deep to see.' She shook her head and tut-tutted at the hopelessness of him and his ilk. 'You!' she added, shouldering me backwards. 'Stop gawping and bring some wood in.'

And here I am wearing the thing, Mum, I say to her in my mind, as neither you nor I would ever have imagined. Here's your thick boy, trying to keep side-on to a wind coming from every way, so it doesn't catch the blessed robe like a sail and blow him off your holy mountain and splat into Beardy Vale.

A terrible glumness settles on me. The thing is too big – not just the robe, which gets between my knees and presses on my shoulders like a pair of filled hods, but the whole damn weather and task and nonsense. *I'm* not Deep – everyone who knows me would laugh at the idea, loud and long.

'I can't do that sort of thing!' I whined in the sickroom. 'I'm not like Flor . . . I can't even—'

189

' "Can't" sets no blossom, boy!' Mum snarled, holding back a cough, looking all witchy with her slept-on hair and her bared teeth. ' "Can't" melts no snow. You get your boots on and take that pack out of my sight. And *now!*'

And I got out, thinking I'd just stay out overnight, go down the old Brimston mine and come back and say I'd done it.

'But she'll know,' I said to myself, in the forest-green, in the mild and ferny places I can hardly remember now. And she will know, if I ever get back – ha!, it's a big *if* – she'll know if I haven't done it all, and done it exactly right. She'll see it in my eyes.

So I clump up, towards the top of the Top, wonky with the robe, drunk with cold and misery.

'Keep your thick head together,' Mum said. 'Say it back to me again.' And she made me say it and say it, the whole long clanging unrhyming poem, tricky as a blade-fish playing the white water, inning and outing and teasing you to beggary. And me realising I'd have to remember it on the bawling Top, with a cowing blizzard at me, with a damn millstone on my shoulders: 'Get off my back! I know it!' I shouted at her, and I slammed out of the house past wheezing Flor.

And now I'm not so sure. *Do* I know it? Do I know it *all?*

I've felt savage the whole way. 'Not my job!' I've shouted at the trees, at the Top's foot, which pokes out low and flattish to lull you before you hit the hard stuff. 'I do the hunting, remember? I bring in the food! I'm one of the dogs, going out to fetch!'

And speaking of dogs, I miss Cuff. I haven't been out

without Cuff at my heel since I was tiny. 'But there's no beasts on the Top, not for this,' Mum said. 'This is a human thing only.'

'I'll tie her up to a tree down the bottom,' I said.

'You'll box her up like I tell you,' said Mum.

The look on Cuff's face when I put her in that box! Pull my heart into fish-bait, why don't you? So I was all aggrieved and misbalanced along the way. Cuff would have stopped me shouting, with her worry, with her wet nose at my hand.

And now I'm in such a rage with this bastard wind, that won't let me get to any kind of rhythm, that scours my face with coldness and bangs my nuisance hair in my eyes, and with the snow, that crusts up the gold on my shoulders and plasters itself to the front so that the mirrors won't shine anyway, awful wet snow that'll soak in and make the wretched burdensome thing even heavier, I tell you—

And all those years of Mum saying I was thick, and people looking on Flor, with his spindly legs and his moon eyes, as the one to treasure and to butter up and to bring soup and sweets to and little gewgaws from Gankly Market! All those years of jealousy, but of relief, too, for who wants to be carrying all these people's hope – who wants to be Deep and different? Yet here I am *anyway* – all the years of putting up with being *not* the one and getting *nothing*, and yet it's me doing the grind, completely without anyone's thanks, only Mum yelling in my head: 'Get a word wrong and you'll know about the flat of my hand, young fella!'

So *many* words! I'm stuck somewhere in the first third of the thing, murmuring the wrong words over and over. I'm not a words person by any imagining – I like places where it's unwise to speak, in a hide beside the grazing field with the deer coming in from all around, among ferns watching a boudoir-bird darting and doubting at my snare. I like to walk in of an evening with a brace of cedar doves, lay them by the pot and go to wash. That way Mum keeps quiet; that's her thanks, her silence. Now there's a wordswoman. Talk you into a hole, my mum would. And she's always right, as well. Wears a person out.

So. I'm here at the summit. Not that it feels like I've arrived, when I have to stagger and throw myself against the ground to keep from blowing away. 'You must stand for part of it,' Mum said, 'but you might have to start off sitting.'

So I get seated, with the robe ends tucked under me, and my face into the wind, so I don't eat hair, and I start the gobbledygook.

I'm fine until I get to the first list. One Father's name dangles off my lips and I can't remember the next. Then comes the wind and smacks me over backwards with what feels like rocks in my face, a clump of snow-slop. 'They won't want you to do this,' Mum said. 'Don't ever think things want to change. It's a battle to make it happen. Now start at the top again.'

So I go back to the head of the Father list and I have another stab at it. Trouble is, our Fathers only had about three different names – then they'd add 'the Seventh', or 'the Strong' or 'with the Askance Eye'. It's a beggar to remember.

But, surprise, I do in the end. And then it's Beasts, which was a list I knew anyway; everyone gets taught the animals when they're little, just for fun. Then come the Mothers – another hard one, all those old witches with their sharp tongues coming out of their sharp brains. And then the Herbage – quite a lot of people know the plants, too, and I knew all of it except the herbs for beauty, which Mum taught me last night. There's only a few of them; I don't know why I didn't learn them before. 'Useful to know for your wife,' Mum grumped, 'or for when you're going after a wife.' Wife? I think of a wife, sometimes. A kind and quiet wife, not Deep, nothing fancy. A wife like me, except rather more beautiful, thanks.

I carve the words out of the icy air with my snow-blown lips. Amazing – I'm getting it all out! It's like Mum's here, coughing and scowling at me in the lamplight, propped up on one elbow. That look on her face stands for no carry-on, no wandering away. 'Put your whole brain to it, boy!' she said, and now I see what she means. Even that part of my brain that's usually there at one side, knocking the rest into line and stopping me moaning against what I have to do, even that part's in on the job, passing me the words, worrying ahead for the next ones.

Now the lists are over and I'm into the wild stuff. *Get up, boy!* says my phantom mum. *You can't command the wind and weather when you're huddled on your bum, however fancy the robe you wear.* So I struggle up, shouting words that I mumbled, embarrassed, in front of Mum last night. They sounded powerfully pompous in our rough little home, but they suit this strong weather. They're something to throw at the wind; words seem like nothing, but they're tiny, fancy, *people's* things. Who cares whether they do anything? What else can we put up against the wind except our tininess and fanciness? What else can the wind put up against us but its big, dumb, howling brute-strength? *So there!*, I tell it with my miniature mouth, my tiny frozen pipe of a throat, my stumbling tongue (and even the stumbling is good, for the wind never stumbles, never goes back and rights itself, don't you see?). *All you've got is your noise – and I've got noise, too! And mine's a thing of beauty!*

On through the verse I go. I'm moving through all the world now, crop and town and ocean and sandhill, river and forest, rock and mist and tarn, describing the springtime we need for each. ('Miss one and I'll lob you,' said Mum. 'Better to say some twice than miss one.') I can't even *hear* the words, except in my head; my ears are full of the hooting and tearing of the wind. A gust nearly thumps me over the edge, and I fall to my hands and knees. The wind drags on the robe, grinding me backwards across the Top's top. I throw myself flat, still shouting; if I keep on, I might get through this alive. But the wind is trying to tell me otherwise. *Shut up and I'll stop*, it says, pounding me with hail-rocks. *Stop now and I'll let you go.*

The wind doesn't know my mother.

I'm glad of the words of that last verse; they save my life. They fill my mind and stop me thinking, *How can a living soul get through this?* They give me a thread to cling to as the storm beats its sodden laundry on me. I get to the end and there is so much strife and thrashing weight against my back, I start the verse again, yelling it into the rock, wrapping my arms around my head against the beating.

Mindless minutes pass. I hang on, I shout, I wait for the

wind's fingernail to lever me off the Top like a scaly-bug egg off a leaf. If I move, it'll only happen sooner: that sickening lift, that awful drop into nothing, that crash, those last seeping few seconds of smashed pain. I've seen a raddle-cat's face in between the two hard bashes it takes to stave in its skull; I think I have an idea; I think I know what's in store.

At least I got the thing done. And done right, hey.

Oof! *This* is the gust that will do it. No – this, *this* is the one. This one's got the lift, this one's got the fingernails – that's right, under the forearms, under the shoulders, flip me up, toss me in the boiling storm, then let me drop—

It's the robe that saves me. Saves my head being stove in like a cat's, anyway.

I wake up rather elegant, in a cradle of rock. The breeze taps my face with a robe-corner. A lazy blueness, from a whole nother age, is spread all above me. A pair of keo-birds twindle slowly up into it, higher and higher to dots, and then gone.

Lovely quiet. I don't want to move.

But things start moving without me. Feels like a new arm, stiff and not quite set in its glue. A lump of a leg, gone dead from lying so funny so long. And then very nervously my head, heavy as a river-rock. Everything hurts, from skin through innards to my aching cold bones.

I'm sitting up, though I don't remember deciding to. The robe is soaked, heavy as plate-armour. I crawl out of it, and fold it after a fashion. The breeze, bright and brisk and icy, is trying to pretend it's not embarrassed about all that carry-on last night. If last night it was; I feel as if I lay there through a full round of seasons, and woke in a whole new life.

I glance down through the clouds and there's Gankly town, embroidered red on its green vale. Gankly's north of Beardy, and the cairn and our home are south. Clutching the lumpish robe to my chest, like an old madman all his worldly goods, I slide and scramble around the mountain.

Even weighted with those stones, the pack has been dragged right across the cairn's clearing. I empty the stones, and stuff the robe in, and lift the whole soggy bundle onto my back.

It's a long, long way down – and quiet, the cautious, damaged quiet that comes after a big blow. I walk alone through the warming world; I step over wet black branches torn to the ground by the wind; I leap from side to side of the brook that yesterday was my dry path upward. All these months the Top's been without colour, but now the winter grass is flushing greenish-gold before my eyes, the rocks are flecked violet and blood-red and patched with bronze lichen, and the sky is a deep, cloudless blue. I did it. I took hold of the mighty millstone of the seasons, and moved it, grinding and squeaking, onward in its circle. I hauled the words out of my memory one by one, and they stilled the winds, and brought this spring.

'Cuff?' I call, when I get home. In the shed, her muffled bark is immediate and mad, and she throws herself about in her box. But no person comes to door or window of the house. Everything is too quiet.

I prepare myself to find Mum and Flor, calm as calm. Everything dies. Look at those Langhorne girls. Look at every deer and cat and bird and fish that ever I hooked or trapped. It's no big thing. I've been so alone these last hours, I can't imagine the aloneness ending, can't imagine other people, their speech, their eyes. That's marvellous stuff, lost to me now.

On the driest grass I can find, I spread out the robe. It's still a feast for the eyes, even after all the feasting I've done on the way down. It's a different kind of feast, not grown by itself from seed or spore, but worked by people, for people's reasons, for people's use.

The house is dark, and smells of dead fire and the nettle-pulp for the coughs. Flor lies very still, his mouth open, his eyes slits of white. He's got the red quilt over him, that we only use for guests; Mum must have struggled to get it onto him, being so sick herself. My little brother, always so thin and pale and smiley. He turned the seasons beautifully for us last year. He did what I did, and I don't know how. I remember it rained on and on, and Mum paced up and down and swore as she peered out the window waiting for him. I remember the little drowned rat that came home in the end, his eyes brilliant with what he'd done, all the fear and seriousness gone from his skinny, joyful frame.

I go over to him, for it's not often in your life you get a good close private look at a dead person; there are always funeral people about, making it rude to stare. I have a good long stare at Flor, long enough for Cuff to stop bothering to bark. Still as a log, still as a stone . . . and then there's a tremor of eyelashes, a glimmer on the eye-whites. I put my face closer and feel the warmth off him. A soft snore comes from the other room and I startle, and nearly laugh out loud. The two of them, both still here! Instead of struggling like before, Flor breathes deeply and silently – now I see the rise and fall of his chest under the motionless quilt.

'You great, soppy fool,' I mutter to myself, sniffing back the sudden tears. 'All they needed was bed-rest, and a bit of nettle.'

Mum is curled up like a possum, her face away from me. I go in, around the bed, with some half-baked notion in my head of waking her, of telling her, of claiming from her some kind of a blessing.

But then I go right off the idea. Her sleeping face is like punched-down bread dough; it's as creased as the rock of Beard's Top, and as polished, with the sweat of her broken fever. She's a sick little old lady – for now, at least. Before she wakes and starts pelting me with accusing questions and making me wish I'd never gone to all the bother. She needs sleep more than anything else. And the spring will come, whether she believes I brought it or not.

The shed smells of dog-pee and wood-damp. It's dark, and I find Cuff's box by following her scratching and whining, the brush of her nose on the splintery wood.

'Cuff, Cuff, my girl!' I whisper.

She throws herself against my side of the box and barks twice.

'Shall we go up to Highfields, shall we?' I murmur, feeling along the bench for the jemmy I left there. 'Shall we get ourselves a snow-hare, you and me, and put it in the pot for the invalids? I think we shall, girl. I think we shall.'

And murmuring so, I ease up the box lid. Before the last nail's free, Cuff pours out the opening into my arms, all tongue and toenails. Then she's in the shed doorway, looking back, her raised paw saying, *When you're quite ready* . . . And beyond her is all the dampness and the dazzle of the first day of spring.

the point of roses

For Finn Lanagan-Jonas, owner and namer
of the original Pumfter

Billy flew into the kitchen. The screen door clapped closed after him.

'You're back,' said Nance.

Corin looked up from the dishes, to the world reflected in the window. The boy was wild and clammy-looking from running, his clothes every which way and filthy, his chest going with his panting. Nance admired him as he passed.

'Just for a minute,' he said. 'I've got to fetch some stuff.'

'What stuff? For what?' barked Corin automatically.

'Just stuff. Any old thing. Three things.' This last was tossed back from halfway down the hall.

The boy rummaged in his room, and rattled. Then he was back in the doorway.

'You need a haircut,' said Corin to the boy's reflection.

'What are you wild lads up to?' said Nance.

'Shai's brother's got psychic powers. We're doing experiments.'

'Psychic powers! Well, well,' said Nance.

'Maybe he can tell you where you dropped that shed key,' said Corin.

'Not that kind of power,' said Billy scornfully.

'Of course, not anything *useful*.'

There was a skilful summoning whistle outside.

'I've got to go,' said Billy, starting for the door.

'Kiss!' Nance commanded.

He darted back, kissed her cheek quickly, and was gone.

Corin was up to his elbows in suds. Nance, at the table in her glasses, went slowly on through the newspaper. She would suck up all the news, but she would never speak to him about it, as if he didn't have ears or something. As if he didn't have a brain to hear with. As if he might not *like* to hear, because reading it himself was such a labour.

'What's the boy got there?' said Corin, putting his forehead to the window. He brought sudsy hands up to block out the other reflections.

'He's got . . .' Nance looked up and dredged the picture of Billy out of her memory. 'He's got Pumfter von Schnitzel, and that ashtray. The one on a stick.'

Ah yes, from the old days, when Corin had pleased himself where he smoked. 'And he's pinched one of those blessed roses on the way out,' Corin said. 'The Zephyr ones. Or whatever silly name they've got.'

Nance licked her fingertip and caught up a corner of the paper. 'Hmm,' she said, reading.

Corin looked over his shoulder at her. 'You're not bothered?'

'Bothered by the rose? He can have a rose. As long as he's not tearing the petals off every bloom.'

'By any of those things. What if he loses that dog thing?'

She looked up at him, dragging her mind back from wherever to hear him. 'He doesn't need it as much as he used to.'

'You said you'd never find another with quite such a look on its face. You said in the whole basket there were no others with that look. It's an accident, the way his eyes were sewn on.'

'What a memory. That was years ago.' Nance looked properly at him now. 'You just don't want him playing with those Traveller kids.'

'My eye, I don't.'

'You're not really so bothered about Pumfter.'

'Maybe not.'

Nance went back to the paper.

Colin sudsed on; plates clanked in the sink and then clacked into the rack. He heard his breath adjusting itself to every shift of his anxiety.

'It's nearly *dark*,' he said.

'It's summer,' said Nance in that *patient* tone he hated. 'It's long evenings. You go out there and let your eyes adjust and see how dark it is.'

'Maybe I should. Maybe I should follow the little bugger and see what they're up to.'

'Maybe.' There she went again. What she meant was, *Of course you shouldn't! Leave the boy to his adventures, you clumsy great berk.*

Corin heaved a sigh. He sneaked a look at Nance's reflection. Was she smiling? He wouldn't put it past her, to have a smile at his expense. Smug cow.

*

'Where is he, then?' asked Billy.

'Up on the hill in the reserve,' said Shai. 'We'll go up and signal when we're near.'

'He can't spy down on us and see?'

'It's all bushy. And he doesn't *want* to cheat, remember. Besides, he'd never guess *this*. What is it?'

'It's an ashtray.'

'Like, for fags?' Shai looked it up and down. 'It's huge.'

'You stand it, beside your armchair.' Billy stood it in the air as they walked. 'Then you tap-tap your ash on the little tray there and *push* the button, and it spins and all goes in underneath, see?'

'It's a marvel. What a thing. Well, I know Jo's never seen such a one. And a toy, there.'

'It's supposed to be a dog.' Billy held Pumfter up and watched him do his work on Shai's face.

'That's got a friendly look. Let me hold him a second —ooh, his flower came away.'

'That's the third thing. It's a rose. My grandma grows them and they win prizes.'

'I thought it were part of the doggy. You were very pretty with your rose, weren't you, doggy? He's a good size. For holding, eh. Or for tucking away here, look. I can carry him?'

'Of course you can. I've got to keep this rose nice. And manage this ashtray, or it'll trip me up. Have we got to go through bushes or anything?'

'We can go around by the walking path. But we've to pick up Castle and Alex first.'

'No, you've not.' Their two forms bobbed darkly up out of the hedge.

'You must have shovelled that dinner,' said Shai.

'We did. Dad said it was disgusting. Alex's made himself sick.'

'Don't talk about it,' said Alex. 'I'll keep it down if I think of something else.'

'He wouldn't miss this, not after I told him about last time,' said Castle to Shai.

'Hopefully we won't get into such trouble,' said Shai. 'Hopefully we're far enough away.'

'In Cottinden's Domain? It's a bloody hike, all right. It'll be dead dark coming home.'

'It'll be worth it. And there'll be a moon.'

By the time they got to the hilltop Billy was just about puffed. No one had helped him with the long-stemmed ashtray or the fragile rose, although Pumfter von Schnitzel had been passed from boy to boy all the way. He was now in Alex's shirt, his kind face poking out between buttons. *It's all right*, he seemed to say to Billy. *None of them are clean, but you can wash me, remember? Just throw me in the machine.*

Jo was idling on the picnic table at the hilltop. Trees crowded behind him. The pinking light in their upper branches glowed also in the pale, grubby cloth of Jo's shirt.

Shai gave his whistle and Jo came alert and called out, in Travellers' language, and Shai called back.

'And bnah bnah blah blah Billy?' said Jo.

'He's here.'

To Billy it was a marvel, that they could switch between one language and another. And a shame and an honour both, that they would stay in his language while he was with them.

'You're set?' Shai called out.

'It's not a matter of *me* being set.' Jo's face moved against the dark trees, searching for some sight of them.

'Well, we've got everything. You can start any time.'

'You got three things?'

'Aye.'

'Choose one, then. Put it forward of you, and keep the others back. Behind a stone or a big tree or something.'

Alex scrabbled Pumfter out of his shirt. The boys all looked to Billy.

'No,' said Billy. 'Let's put this flower first, before it spoils or gets stepped on or something.'

'Here.' Shai ushered him towards a boulder covered with picnickers' graffiti. 'INDIA 4 STORM – remember that. Put the others behind there.'

'Why?' Billy laid Pumfter down and propped the ashtray against some stones so that it wouldn't roll. 'I mean, why remember? We'll be right here, won't we?'

'Maybe not. There might be a bit of travelling involved. A bit of wandering.'

'Oh.' Billy had thought it would be more like a show, where they sat and rested and watched.

'So. Put that forward on the ground there. But not anywhere Jo can see it.'

'I can't see nothing in those bushes,' said Jo. 'I'm not even trying.'

'It's forward. We're ready,' said Shai. 'Do your thing.'

'Yer, shake yer booty,' said Castle.

'Ah, shhh!' said Shai. 'You've got to be serious.'

'I can't help it. It's funny.'

'You spoil this, I'll whack you so hard,' hissed Alex.

'Quiet in there, then,' said Jo from the clearing. 'I can't go with all that racket.'

'Can't go? What's he doing, working up a good crap? Ow.'

'Shut up, you meelmeek.'

'All right, I'm going,' Jo sang out.

'Where to, is he going?' Billy murmured to Shai.

'Off away to the inside of his own head,' said Shai. 'He's got to use the psychic place. It's right in the middle, he says. In his lizard brain.'

They waited. For quite some minutes they were four boys crouched in bushes, one boy on a picnic table, and a fragrant rose in between. Evening hung above them, its high, cool note singing on and on, over the crickets' pulsing. Birds flew home and put themselves to bed here and there. Some land creature moved, Billy couldn't tell how far away, or what size, shrew or badger or wandering pony.

Then Jo got up and, with fluid movements that were not his own, stepped from table to bench to ground. He groped at the two buttons of his pinkish-whitish shirt, undid them by hauling rather than finger-work, dragged the shirt off over his head and stood there frowning, swinging his face blindly.

''S around here somewhere,' he said in a deep, drugged voice.

He lifted his face to listen. Rose-ness welled up out of the evening and rushed at them. Alex gave a shout. A sweet-scented shock hit Billy, a velvety punch. Down the slope he tumbled, alone in a storm of blooms, streaked and scraped with darker leaves. His lungs struggled, his skin dissolved, his thoughts turned to vapour as the rose essence passed through, roaring.

Corin was at the bins. He felt it coming as you feel a wave in the sea; it sucked stuff away, ahead of itself. Corin gripped the rim of the council wheelie-bin, tried to stand firmer on the bumpy ground of the bin yard.

It hit, a powerful buffet of sweet air. It tossed his hair, rocked him, rocked the near-full bin. It must have rocked the roses. It must have stripped Nance's roses from their stems, to carry such a scent.

But there were no petals on the streaming air. Corin ran against the wind, blundered out of the yard and around the house. He must see what had happened.

At the corner of the house, the wind stopped him, like rose-scented tarpaulin stretched across his path. But only he was blown and bewildered; nothing else moved, not a twig, not a leaf, not a flower. All Nance's garden stood serene in the dying summer evening.

But along the fence the rosebushes were jagged black candelabra. The roses brightened in the bloom wind, the rose wind, big soft rose-lamps propped among the rough leaves and the thorns. They shone and they shed— was it a smoke? It was like dust, or tiny seeds, or tiny, numerous, distant stars gone to milk on the sky, or like the curls of grainy steam from your soup or your tea. This stuff purled and streamered across the lawn to Corin; he breathed it and it filled his brain, which had broken open when the wind first hit him.

Her *name* is Rose, he thought dizzily, and knew he had hit upon something.

Nostrils flared, mouth wide to keep catching the wind, he stumbled after the strand of thought, back along the house wall.

He saw Nance through the screen. The white tail of her hair was blown forward over one shoulder; hair-wisps danced around her face, which was all opened out and smoothed of its lines and thoughts by surprise. The newspaper lay flat on the kitchen table where Nance had pushed it back; it was unmoved by the wind. But the rose catalogue underneath – Nance held some of the catalogue pages down, but others rattled back and forth in the breeze, and the photographed roses were smudged on the pages, and shed sweet crimson, velvet mauve and soft ivory across the kitchen air.

'Rose!' He called her true-name through the screen. Because – he would never be able to explain to her! – she was the source of it. It was she who blew the rose-coals to brightness, it was she who, in the first place, had had the idea of the roses. It was she – it was the children all over again! He saw that, too! He had fumed and raged against each pregnancy, and snarled and boiled and beat at the children as they grew, and railed at her for enslaving herself to them – instead of to him! But there she'd been, swelling and dreaming and knitting and working and reading to them and making their little foods and fending him off them, all according to the garden plan in her head. She had had the children plotted out just so, as if on sheets of squared paper, and she had kept him out, just as she'd not let him do a spadeful of digging or bring a barrowload of bricks to edge the rose-bed – because he snarled and sneered so, because, allowed in, his anger would have thrashed about and damaged the whole project of the roses, of the children, of the garden.

'I'm sorry about the roses!' He felt as if he shouted, but it came out a child's cry, afraid the night would hear and descend on him. The wind softened; the rose-colours were fading in the kitchen, Nance's hair settled and she looked about, for herself and for him, the speaker beyond the door-screen.

'It just seemed so old-womanish,' he said falteringly, trying to get *some* words out before the wind, the thought, entirely went. 'I just wanted you to stay my girl—'

And it was gone. The last colours slid off the catalogue pages and trickled to invisibility across the table.

Nance stood up and scraped the chair back. 'Of course!' She came around to the door. She was laughing, but not unkindly. 'So that you could stay a boy, and all the girls still want you! Well, what kind of life is that, on and on and on? What is the use of that?'

'I don't know,' he said, frightened. 'But I didn't know . . . what was the use of roses, either. I couldn't see the point before, you see—'

She pressed her mouth to the screen, and he met it with his. Their warmths warmed the mesh. She put her hand up beside her face, and he matched it with his hand, and they were there for a moment, like reflections of each other, yet quite different. Quite different from each other, yet meeting at the mouth.

The other boys talked in Traveller, bubbles and scraps of noise. Billy lay on the hillside, gripping the ground with his hands, with the skin of his back, with the back of his head.

Above him everything swirled in the aftermath, and a few stars sang, restoring the world to stillness.

'Hum-humnah-Billy?'

'Wait,' he said sharply.

'Oof. Arf,' said Castle. 'I'm all gone to petals and come back again.'

Yes, thought Billy, they're about the words for it.

'How does Jo go?' he said. It was hard to shape his mouth around all that meaning.

'Me?' said Jo, in his normal voice. 'I'm all right. I'm *very* all right. Don't worry about me.'

'It makes him feel good,' said Shai. 'It gives him jollies. He'll be impossible, these next few days.'

Jo clapped and rubbed his hands. Both sounds seemed to happen right inside Billy's head. 'So what else have you got for me?' he said.

'What was that one, first?' said Castle.

''Twas a rose. An old Bourbon rose called "Zéphirine Drouhin", soft mid-pink in colour, with a strong fragrance. A little fussy in its habits and prone to black spot. The absence of thorns makes this rose ideal for children's play areas, and—'

'All right, give it a rest,' said Shai. 'Get back on your table.'

'No, I'm down now. I'm ambillant. I'm good.'

'Well, turn around, then.'

'I tell you, I can't see. It's like a black curtain – well, dark grey, with branches and trunks.'

'Turn around so *we* know. This is a scientific test.'

'Sheesh, can we wait a bit?' muttered Alex in a mooshed voice. He must have his face in his hands.

213

'Not too long,' said Shai, 'He's on his roll now. Billy, get that rose back and put out the next object.'

Billy pushed the spinning part of his brain into a corner. He bent and retrieved the rose from the bushes. He sniffed deeply of it as he took it to the INDIA 4 STORM rock, but no, it was only the merest hint of the rose-ness that had passed over and through him. It was nearly nothing in comparison, yet it was something enough to send him mad with sniffing and trying and yearning, if he let it.

Pumfter regarded him kindly, and he patted the dog's worn cloth head. Then he laid the rose beside Pumfter and took out the ashtray.

It clinked and rattled as he pushed it into the bush.

'It's a cowbell; that was easy,' said Jo.

'Don't be cheeky,' said Shai.

Jo paced back and forth. His chest was narrow and bruised looking. 'Are we ready, then? Are we good?'

'Shut up, Jo. Alex, how are you coming?'

'I'm a bit better.'

'What about you, Billy?'

'I'll be all right,' said Billy stoutly.

'Right, Jo. We're ready for you.'

A jittery silence fell. The forest sounds flowed into it.

Jo stood poised, as if about to take a step, or to bend forward and vomit.

'Gawd,' said Castle under his breath, 'what will he make of *this*?'

'He doesn't *make* anything,' said Shai. 'He told me. He just connects. The object uses him to find, I dunno, something else. Something bigger. Oops—'

Jo had swung away from them, had started down the far slope.

'Quick, after him!' said Shai. 'Sometimes he whistles along. Billy, you bring the object.'

Billy caught up with them at the forest edge. Jo moved on ahead, indistinct as a marsh-candle, as quietly as if he were flowing around the trees, floating over the ground, and the others thudded after him, grunting and swearing.

'Where is the bugger?' said Shai. 'I've lost him.'

'Down there,' said Billy. 'Headed for the brook. See?'

'Good man.'

When they reached Jo, he had dropped his pants and belt on the thin crescent of sand. He stood up to his calves in the shallows of a pool, which a lacework of tiny waterfalls spilled into. A star-reflection rocked jauntily over the ripples he made.

'Watch him,' whispered Shai. 'He can't swim. When he's like this he thinks he can, though. Fly, too, sometimes.'

Jo stood, bent as if cold, his hands dark on his knees. He turned and looked straight at them, his face skull-like and awful in the darkness. 'Ssshhh,' he said.

'Think about the thing, the object!' said Shai in a terrified whisper.

Billy locked his mind onto the image of a younger, red-haired Grandpa Corin. This Corin laid his cigarette in the ashtray, ignoring the fascinated Billy at his knee. He resettled his bum in the big armchair, hunched over the form guide. The cigarette smoke went up in straight lines to a certain level, then began to bend and twine. The tiny Billy itched, stuffed full of one desire: *Press the button, Grandpa. Spin it away. Before Nance comes and finds me and snatches me up, and says, 'Come away from that dirty thing. Leave your Grandpa to his smells, why don't you—'*

Jo straightened, and reached his skinny arms up, and spread his fingers, and gathered something down on himself, down on them all. It blotted out the sky in an instant. It crushed the boys flat to the ground, and filled their minds and mouths with ashes.

Corin pushed Nance away.

'It's coming again!' He tried to see it beyond the walls of the bright kitchen.

'You think?' said Nance hopefully. Her lips were pinked from kissing him. Her whole face had come unset from its folds and habits; from here it might age any number of different ways.

'It's at Cowper Fen with the Travellers now—' Fearfully Corin searched the ceiling. 'Though it's not from there; it's from beyond there. It's wobbling the church steeple! It'll be here soon, it'll be in the garden—!'

A cindery blast pushed him against the cupboards and the door. Who was he? Who was that old lady, clutching the table-edge? She was someone's grandmother; she had one of those strong, capable, sexless bodies in the middle of all those wind-whipped clothes. But she would die anyway; he knew it.

He was running in the night. Things banged and obstructed his knees; things shattered in his wake. Tiny cries came after him. 'Don't call out like that!' he muttered. 'Don't go right back to a *baby*!'

The bin-yard wall caught him in the ribs, smacked the breath out of him, lashed his head forward. The ground lit up orange. Hot air attacked his face, swooped down his throat and choked him.

The yard was a pit, full of magma that turned and split and sank into itself. In the time before the electric, Corin had gathered and stamped years' worth of ashes, to make the yard floor; now these had all come alive again, and stank, and melted. The plastic bins drooped, and the raised letters on the council bin – NO HOT ASHES – glowed in the moments before the bin collapsed and was enfolded. Flames came and went across the mass, like runners of grass, only of fire.

Corin hung coughing, aghast, over the wall. New knowledge bounded through him, like a herd of black bulls caught along a narrow street and panicking: this ashy wind that pinned him here, it went nowhere; it blew only from one giant hollowness to another. He, Rose, everyone they knew, everyone they had ever known, every *thing* – put together, they were no more than one of those white sparks, there for a moment on the breast of the turning magma, and then engulfed and gone utterly.

'Corin! Corin!' she cried from the house. At any other time it would have started him running, it would have flicked him like a switch it was so raw, so full of fear and sorrow, so unlike the Nance he knew and wanted, the Nance he relied on to take the brunt of him. But now, with fumes in his eyes and the fire bawling and stretching and being consumed below him – *What can she do for me? Or I for her? All we can do is scrabble at each other, moan our fear at each other as we go down.*

Afterwards, Nance found him crouched by the wall, staring

unblinking at the new-risen moon, coated like herself in the finest of fine grey ash.

'That's an ashtray, that one,' said Joe cheerily. 'Made of chrome-plated steel. A mechanism, activated by a Bakelite knob, spins the ash and cigarette butts into the bulb below, where any remaining spark is extinguished by oxygen starvation.'

'*Mechanism*,' said Shai through chattering teeth. '*Extinguished*. He don't get those words from our family.'

Billy didn't know how Shai could talk at all. Billy himself had died just now; he had felt himself choking, and death had twirled his brain out of his head and mulched it into some substance that would be used again and again, to make ants or trees, or maybe other people, or maybe gases for some other planet, and all Billy-ness had left the world forever.

Now here he was, back, boy in wood, so frightened he didn't know how he was going to get home to Nance and Grandpa Corin's. Jo was cackling and prancing naked in the shallows; the others were huddled around Billy, all warmth and gulping breath. Alex's ear was pearly and intricate in the faint light; the very grubbiness of the hand, the very bittenness of the nails that came up to scratch it made Billy feel weepy and full of wonder. At the same time, he held in his guts a black cannonball of fear; it sat and sucked all possible movement out of his body.

'Come on, you.' Jo capered around them, scattering cold drops of brook-water. 'One more!'

'Put your clothes on, you geet,' growled Castle. 'You look like a death-doll, all head and willy.'

218

Jo laughed insanely and danced off to obey.

The four others risked looking at each other. Thank heaven, thought Billy. He had thought his own face must be peeled back to the skull; now he knew, seeing Castle's wary eyes and Alex's teary ones, that he looked like his old, young self.

'That was *horrible!*' whimpered Alex, and a hiccoughing breath made the juices rattle in his nose.

'I'm sorry,' said Billy. 'The ashtray was a bad idea. But I used to *like* it. You said—' He turned to Shai. 'You said, pick things that *mean* something. So I did. I didn't know it would—' He broke off so as not to cry, waving his hands about.

'It's all right,' said Shai. 'You weren't to know. How were you to know? Who'd have thought *that*, of an ashtray? My oath.'

They all four turned. Jo was trying to put his second leg in his shorts; he hopped sideways on the sand, bent headless over the task. Castle shuddered and turned away.

'I don't want to do another one,' said Alex. 'I just want to be at home. But I don't want to walk home through this forest – it's all shadows and noises.'

'Well, you'll have to, won't you?' snapped Castle.

Billy felt the same as Alex. What were they going to do? he wondered.

'Wait a bit,' said Shai, patting Alex's shoulder. 'Let it fade a bit.'

'It'll *never* fade,' Alex whispered. 'I'll *never* forget.'

'You will, too,' said Shai. 'Just like you forget a bad dream.'

'I don't forget those, either,' said Alex, weeping. 'I lie there

219

going over and over it in my head, and trying not to go back to sleep and have it again. And sometimes I *do* go to sleep, and I *do* have it again—'

'Shut up or I'll slap you, Alex,' said Castle. 'You're working yourself up. Now stop it.'

Alex stopped, and mopped his eyes miserably.

'Look,' said Shai. 'The moon's coming up. That'll be daylight, practically.'

Except that moon-shadows are blacker than sun ones, thought Billy. They can hide more *things*, to jump out at you. But he didn't say it; he wasn't about to frighten himself worse.

Nance went to Corin through the broken flowerpots. He was against a wall, and beyond the wall was the grave – she smelled its greasy sweetness. He was all bones wrapped thinly in flesh, then loosely in cloth; his hair was white scraps floating from his speckled scalp in the moonlight.

'Come inside, Corin,' she scolded in her crone's voice. 'Look at you! You're all over ashes!' How had they got to be so old, she and he? It seemed to Nance that they had held each other in a death-clasp all these years, meanly squeezing until every scrap of colour was gone from skin and hair, until their voices held no juice and their eyes too much. It seemed a dreadful desperate togetherness, this marriage, quite biological and loveless; she had watched frogs mating once, and it was like that, like a long, hard clinch with spasms of wrestling, now sinking, now floating, and all the while the eyes looking out, frog eyes, showing nothing. And here she was, kicking shards out of the way with her frog feet, and shaking

220

the ash off his shirt with her frog hands – no, with her old-woman's hands, all worn and creased – whoever would have thought moonlight could be so cruel? Look at them! She snatched them off him and hid them from herself.

She reached for something habitual to say. 'I'll run you a bath,' she brayed at him. 'Corin?'

He would not look up. She crouched in front of him, leaning against the tomb wall.

'Corin, Corin.'

The moonlight gave him a great and glowing brow. His eyebrows sizzled along its rim. The bulls thundered from his skull-holes into hers, on and on. She could do nothing, for herself or for him; she couldn't even blink. His eyes' black beams had caught and locked her.

Slowly, carefully, chivvied by jolly Jo, keeping hold of each other's shirts and elbows, and Alex and Castle holding hands because they were brothers and that was all right, they crept back up the hill. Billy kept himself going by thinking: As soon as I'm up top, I'll tell them, No more. I'll take Pumfter and I'll go home. No, I'll *leave* Pumfter. They can do what they want with him; they can bring him back to me tomorrow.

They reached the clearing. Jo climbed up and sat cross-legged on the table, grinning in the moonlight.

'Don't be *creepy*,' said Castle.

'Fetch the last one. Go on. I'm readier than ready.'

'That's obvious.'

Billy didn't feel so bad after the climb. And now he didn't fancy going home on his own, so much. So he went with Shai to the INDIA 4 STORM rock.

Shai picked Pumfter up and hugged him. Billy had to stop himself snatching at the dog: That's *mine*! His rage was like the stiffness that happened in his throat when he was about to be sick; he swallowed down hard on it, and laid the ashtray next to the rose.

'Here, you put him out.' Shai handed Pumfter to him, and Billy felt ashamed of the rage – Shai had been through the nightmare too; he needed Pumfter just as much as Billy did.

Billy took a draught of Pumfter's friendly face in the moonlight. He remembered when Pumfter had been as big as another person in bed next to him. Although he hadn't kissed the dog for years, he knew exactly the feel of that felt nose, those rough seams. He didn't need to kiss him.

'All right,' he said, and went up into the bushes and put Pumfter there. Then he huddled with Alex and Castle and Shai on the slope, watching Jo nervously.

'Go on, then, Jo,' called Shai, then added very softly to the others, 'Now, think about that nice doggy.'

Alex's free hand crept into Billy's. Billy went still, feeling grateful and responsible and unworthy.

And then the feelings squashed themselves, and their insides leaked everywhere. The sky opened up in a wide, tooth-edged smile, and a sour, loving fog filled the clearing. It thickened and warmed and became shaggy. Jo jumped about trying to grab handfuls of it; the others sank unconscious to the ground. The dog-ness nosed around them for a moment, nudged Billy, gave Jo's tiny hand a lick; then it sprang from the top of Cottinden's Hill and exploded into the wider world.

*

Corin broke gaze with Nance to look up. This third thing sopped up moon and starlight as it came; it had a different darkness from the sky's – damp, grey-brown, ragged at its leading edge.

He half-rose to meet it. The mist, which was the exact temperature of his own skin, took away his balance, lifted him off his feet. He tumbled, slowly, over and over, until he fetched up against some wall or planet. He sank away under the smell of dog-fur and dog-breath and wet, new grass, and was nowhere for a while.

The clink of flowerpot pieces brought him back, the breathing of that woman Rose, the paving under his hip, the wall under his boot; the fact that there was a house nearby and that it was their house, his and the woman Rose, the woman Nance's; the fact that every object in it, and in this garden, stood clean-edged, itself, and known to him.

They were walking along the path; they were helping each other along the path. They were very weak; they were a little hilarious with their weakness. Their legs were stumps and their arms were lumps and their heads were great heavy pots of brains, fitfully electric. Corin's ears seemed to be stuffed with cotton wool. The door – the thin slapping screen door that his hands knew every nail and board of, the screen with its summertime load of moths and lacewings – Rose opened it and admitted them to the house, and it felt like some sort of ceremony.

He was at the table trying to explain, talking loudly, clumsily through the cotton wool. *And being angry was a kind of paint,* he bellowed, *and I splashed it all over everything, and everything looked the same. Everything was just something that would make me angry again. Because-because-because-because . . . All those becauses, on and on – for years, Nance! For my whole life!*

Nance laughed and brought tea – in a cup!, gold-rimmed!, instead of his bitten-looking old mug that he might have insisted on. He rubbed the scarred table around the saucer wonderingly. *Do you think I've had some kind of stroke?*

Well, if you have, we both have. Her voice was woolly and distant.

Her hair was bright white and wiry, and ashes and a leaf were caught in it. Her face was as old as his and laughing, and her eyes! My goodness, all their lives were in there. He would have to look more. He would have to ask her things—

And then, with a slap of door and a swirl of moths, here came the boy.

Billy! said Nance – even through the wool Corin heard how much was in her voice, was in the name. But by the fact that she left her body facing him as she turned to speak, he understood that she was sharing, not trying to claim the boy all to herself.

You're asleep on your feet, my darling! she said.

Billy stood the ashtray on the floor to free up a hand. He closed the door properly behind him. He came to the table and laid the rose there.

I borrowed that, he said, hugging the toy dog to his stomach. *It's still good. Maybe you can put it in one of those special vases, the ones for one flower.*

A bud vase? And Nance was up getting one.

Billy kept his gaze on the rose, and Corin looked him up and down. He felt he had never seen this boy before; he didn't know what to do with him besides beleaguer him.

He made his voice very low so that Billy would not mistake him. *How did the experiments go?*

Billy gave one eye a sketchy rub. *Well, he guessed everything.* His hair was dull with cobwebs and sweat.

He's good, then? Corin felt as if he were walking out onto water, using small steps, heel-to-toe, freezing the water with his feet as he went, to make something strong enough to walk on. *He's got the powers?*

Billy looked at him. Corin thought, It's possible I've not met eyes with this boy before. And how old is he? Ten? Twelve? I should know what ten and twelve look like. I should know, from my own children.

He's got too much powers, said Billy. *Says his mum, anyway; she says he's getting too good. She says him and Shai are like babies with a box of bombs. She's so angry. She's sending Jo to the You-Crane to learn from her uncle. That's a country.*

The Ukraine? I've heard of it.

Nance brought the rinsed bud vase to the table and put the rose in it.

I really need a bath, Billy said to her. Then he blinked. *So do you! And you too, Grandpa Corin. What've you been doing to get so dirty?*

They thought about that. Then Corin said gravely, *I put the bin out.*

Nance laughed. *Yes, and . . . and a bit of a wind came up.*

225

Billy looked from face to face. *I told Shai Cottinden's Hill wasn't far enough. Nowhere we could walk to would be.*

You've been all the way to Cottinden's Hill? Nance looked horrified.

I know they felt it at Cowper Fen, Billy said to Corin. *That's why their mum came and met us.*

I think they might have felt it in the Ukraine, said Corin. *I hope that uncle felt it, and comes running.* He finished his tea.

Another? said Nance.

Yes, please.

The empty cup gleamed in Corin's paw.

I know that's fancier than you're used to, Nance apologised, bringing the pot.

It's good. Corin clinked the cup onto its saucer. *It's fine.*

His ears popped and the cotton wool was gone from them. The tea clucked and pattered into the cup. 'And then I'll get the bath on,' said Nance. 'But you'll want a smackle of something to eat, Billy. A round of sandwiches?'

'You go up,' said Corin. 'I can do that.'

She looked at him doubtfully. But he knew, if he let her feed the boy this time, tonight might as well not have happened.

'I'll make him one of my slabs,' he said in the new low voice. 'That'll fill him.'

She smoothed her hair and went. He heard the sounds of Billy climbing into the chair right to the walls of the kitchen, and of Nance's feet on the stairs reverberating to the edges of the house, and beyond that was the garden and the summer night in all its size, with all its traffic of creatures and breezes

226

and brooks and planetary light. And here he was in the middle of it, for the moment, in this house, in this room, moving from here to there gathering bread, gathering cheese and sausage and pickle, knife, board, plate – though he was not, himself, in any way, hungry at all.

acknowledgments

The author acknowledges the following sources of ideas, images and references for these stories:

* Jack Dunbar for the title *black juice*
* Adrian Denyer for the cat bringing home a different creature every night ('Perpetual Light')
* Louis Creagh for hugging the elephant's leg ('Sweet Pippit')
* Janice Dancey for the phrase 'hairy story' ('Wooden Bride')
* the Linstead family of Perth for the word 'bonty' ('Singing My Sister Down')
* *National Geographic* for the picture of a woman skinning monkeys ('Yowlinin')
* the SBS programme 'Global Village' for tar-pits ('Singing My Sister Down') and for children making mud-jeeps ('House of the Many')
* Paddy Doran, Mike Waterson and The House Band for the song 'Seven Yellow Gypsies' from their album *October Song* © 1998 Green Linnet Records Inc. ('My Lord's Man')
* Years 5 and 6 of 1999, Geelong Grammar School, at

workshops with whom 'Yowlinin' and 'Rite of Spring' were
begun

* the magazine *Modern Bride*, the misreading of whose title
gave rise to 'Wooden Bride'

Thanks to Eva Mills, Jodie Webster and Rosalind Price for
editorial help with this collection, and to Rowena Lindquist,
Marianne de Pierres, Tansy Rayner Roberts and Maxine
McArthur for their valuable input at the inaugural wRiters
On the Road (ROR) workshop at Montville, Queensland, in
October 2001.